"YOU WILL BE SORRY"

## Acknowledgments

This book is a work of fiction and is from my imagination and places I have visited and are not intended to resemble any actual persons.

I would like to thank my family and friends for all their support. I couldn't have done it without your help.

## Prologue

He was the life and sole of the party, enjoying an evening out with his fiancé Susie and work colleagues; and their partners.

Jack was responsible for the men in his team as the leader. They all worked for an internet company, laying fibre cable and Jack' role was to deal with the customers and organised things to prevent too much disturbance.

There was Colin, he was in his early 50s, bold, carrying a few extra pounds. His wife Ruth was around 48, very shy, quite attractive. Slightly overweight but Jack thought womanly curves.

Then there was Eddie he was 25 he had a young girlfriend, Ella, blonde very curvy and besotted with Eddie. He was athletically built and loved his tattoos.

Also, Peter who had been married for 7 years and Lisa his wife, she was no oil painting, but Jack thought to himself you don't look at the mantle when you are stoking the fire. Peter had had bad acne as a teenager which had left his face badly pitted and red. Still Lisa seemed content with him. Jamie was their apprentice; he came on his own and lastly there was Derek he was married to Pauline and had been for 20 years. He scrubbed up well and so did his wife. She obviously worked out and had a sparkle in her eye. They had two kids who were now at uni.

They were all in a local club with live music, the atmosphere was electric with dancing, drinking. Everyone was having a wonderful time. Jack was plying them with drinks and flirting with the ladies.

He asked Colin if it was ok to dance with Ruth.

"It's not up to me, Ruth can make up her own mind."

"Come on Ruth, I will be gentle." She reluctantly took his hand. Jack squeezed her hand as to reassure her and led them to the dance floor just as the music changed to a slow dance.

Ruth hesitated, trying to return to their seats.

"Come-on Ruth you deserve a bit of fun." With that he took her in his arms and started moving around the floor. After a while Ruth began to relax and seemed to enjoy herself. They chatted about trivial things and the music came to an end.

"Come on one more dance Ruth."

She smiled then excepted? Lucky the music remained slow so Jack took her in his arms again. This time he held her close, very close. Ruth was too embarrassed to mention this fact and assumed this was normal behaviour and to mention it would make her feel foolish.

Jack was relying on this and knew he could manipulate her to his will. He ran his hand up and down her back and could feel her responding. It could be all the drink he had been buying her but he knew that this was a good start.

They went back to their table; Ruth sat next to Colin and excepted a drink from him.

Jack sat the other side of Ruth and grabbed his drink. He chatted with the others while he placed his hand on Ruth's knee, giving it a gentle squeeze. Ruth went rigid for a split second but didn't remove his hand. Jack took this as a sign and gradually moved his hand up towards her thigh. Again, she drew in a slight breath but didn't stop him. All the while Jack wasn't looking at her but chatting away. This was so thrilling for Jack; he loved this beginning of the chase and he knew she would be very grateful for the attention he would give her. He thought an older woman would crave some excitement, and he would do that given the chance.

The following Monday at work they had moved to a new address and was setting up to lay cable for 6 properties in a small hamlet. Everything was going well then Jack said he had to go back to the yard to fetch some items and left them to continue. Instead, he heads towards Colins home. He hoped Ruth would be there, he wanted to continue what he started.

When he pulled up outside, he noticed her car was in the drive, this was to be his lucky day. He rang the bell and waited; it could go two ways but he hoped it would work in his favour.

Ruth opened the door and was shocked to see Jack.

"Jack, is everything ok? Has Colin had an accident?"

"No, sorry I didn't mean to scare you. I was close and needed the loo. Do you mind?"

"Um, no, come in."

She stepped aside and he headed towards the bathroom. He had been to their home a few times so knew the layout.

When he came out, he found her in the kitchen.

"Would you like a coffee?"

She didn't want to ask him, but this is what she usually did when he called. The difference was Colin was always there with her.

"Cheers, that would be great."

Ruth was feeling a little awkward, she put the kettle on and with her back to Jack tried to make small talk. Jack slid up behind her and placing his hands on her hips pulled her up against his growing groin. As she sighed, he knew she was his.


He was at her door again. She had told him not to call anymore, why wouldn't he listen to her?

"Come on darling, let me in." he shouted through the letter box.

"Go away."

"Tell me to my face." He paused a moment. "Please, you owe me that."

Was she caving in; he knew she would. He could be so persuasive; she was the other side of the door breathing softly?

"Come on Kitten, please."

She opened the door a little and peered out.

"You have to go; he will be back soon."

"Darling, I know he won't, he is picking up cable for me and delivering to a new site, he won't be back for a couple of hours." He ran a finger up and down her arm, then placed his hand on her hip. Gently he gripped her and pulled her up against his firm body. God, she had to say no but she couldn't, he knew which buttons to push.

As his hands cupped her ass and pulled her even closer, she moaned into his neck, his fingers lowered and cupped her sweet spot.

She was lost, she opened the door fully and led him in closing the door behind him.

Across the road they were being watched. Hidden in a clump of trees no one would know anyone was watching. It had been only three days of watching before he turned up at her door. This man was so predictable. He was following his same routine he had followed in the previous dalliances.

"Your time is soon to be over, make the most of it."

It was time to leave the shadows of the trees, walking away quietly, no one was the wiser.

"I won't let you ruin another relationship." Walking past the house they were unaware of what awaited them.

# Chapter 1

"Come on ladies, keep up." Tom was trying to keep everyone motivated and working as a team. This was proving to be difficult as two women seemed to have their own ideas and were heading across the field instead of keeping with the group.

He was running metal detecting days and this was the first in this area, he needed to give them a great day so they would recommend it.

When he came home one day and told his wife he had handed in his notice and was setting up his own business, she wasn't pleased at all, so he had a lot to prove.

Karen was one of the two women wondering with her friend and work colleague Helen. She had won a day's metal detecting in a raffle for two, so asked her if she would like to join her. Helen thought it could be fun, she had always loved digging up the garden as a child looking for clues and making up stories of crimes that might have been committed. She had known she wanted to join the force from an early age.

She was good at her job; DCI Robert Downton would say you had a good eye for detail and that was something you needed in this profession. Helen was in her early thirties; she was married with a daughter and her husband worked from home so was happy to be a house husband.

She was a stunning brunet with a slim figure, but she would give unwanted attention a wide birth. All Helen needed to do was give then a look and they left with their tails between their legs. When the DCI was starting his team, he chose PC Karen Broad to join the them as she had shown promise in the previous case. Karen was ambitious and contributed a great deal to the team. She was around 5ft 2in and had a rounded figure. This didn't mean she was unfit; it was just her DNA; her mother was short and thick set and she followed after her and had her dads' brown eyes. They were searching, inquisitive and caring when needed, she was a friend you could rely on.

There was a team of eleven people on this day's course. 8 women and 3 men. Tom would have liked twelve but one guy cancelled in the last minute.

The instructor was named Tom Mansfield. He was around 35, and looked tired and drawn in the face. He had a lot of worry and stress. His partner and wife Clare didn't seem very interested in being there. They had the introductions at the beginning of the day, in the group they found out 4 girls had been friends for years and were looking for new experiences to enjoy together. The remaining were a varied collection of characters.

While Karen and Helen were away from the main group, they chatted about the case they had just closed. It had been quite a puzzle as one of the bodies had been dead for 20 years. There were so many secrets and lies.

Down the other end of the field a group were getting excited, they were all on their hands and knees scraping away at the edge of the field.

"I wonder what they have found?" asked Karen.

"Probably something the organiser has buried, come on let's see what it is." They walked over to the group.

"It's got to be quite big." Said Helen as they saw the whole group scratching away the earth.

"Come on tell us what you buried." Asked the tall lanky guy who was called Harry.

"I haven't buried anything." Replied Tom.

"It's probably a piece of farm machinery." Said Clare.

"Oh, how disappointing."

They still continued to scrape away the soil and it soon became clear that it was large and oblong in shape.

"What metal are we detecting?" asked Helen.

Tom passed his detector over the area.

"It's tin, I would say."

As they continued it became clear it was some kind of large oblong shaped container.

"It's big." said one of the girls.

"Yes, I could get in it, do you think it will be full of coins?" said one of the others.

Helen was looking at Karen and thinking the same thing. What if there was a body in it?

"Guy's, I hate to break up your fun, but I think we better call in the police to look at this. So can you all stand back."

"Who put you in charge." said Tom.

"I did." Helen presented her badge. "P C Helen Johnson and this is P C Karen Broad."

This took him back a pace.

"Sorry, what do you want me to do?"

"You can keep everyone back please. Karen, you phone the gov?"

"Sure thing."

"No one is to leave and please do not send messages on your phones, in case this is something of a police matter."

They were grumbling together about being bossed around.

Tom asked the reluctant team to follow him back to the make shift carpark alongside the road.

Karen explained to her gov about what they may have found and that they hadn't opened it. DCI Robert Downton decided he wouldn't call the forensic team yet as it could be just a farmer burying rubbish. While they waited the girls carefully removed the excess soil from around the vessel, so as to prepare for closer inspection.

He arrived about 30 minutes later.

"I can't leave you girls for 5 minutes before you sniff out another problem." Said Robert. They walked together toward the discovery.

"Tom thinks it is possibly farm machinery, but I'm not sure about that."

"What makes you think otherwise?"

"Well, if you wanted to bury rubbish, why go to the trouble of getting a large tin vessel."

"They could be chemicals."

"That's illegal."

"True, well here put these on Helen, and Karen, I want you to take pictures of our progress, just in case we find something..." Robert handed Helen a pair of gloves.

Between the two of them they were lucky it wasn't locked and didn't take too much pricing to open.

"Wow." Helen stepped back.

"That's not what I expected." Said Robert.

There were watches, phones, cameras and jewellery all thrown in together, it looked like they may have been put in the box in a hurry.

"Well at least it's not a body this time gov.," said Helen.

"True, I think we better get forensic down here now, to see if there are any prints to identify who put it all in here." He walked a little way to get a signal then made the call.

While Karen continued to take photos of the evidence, Robert asked Helen to get the information of the land owner from Tom, so they could get some details of the surrounding area.

The field was hidden away from the road, there was a wooded area on her right as she walked down the track towards the make shift carpark. To her left was the open field in which they had been searching. When she got to the end of the track she turned to her right and walked over to the group; she could hear them discussing their find.

There was three of the lads and two women. The lad that was most vocal was Harry he had been keen to be the centre of all conversation.

"Yea, but we found it we should have a finder's fee." They were nodding and muttering their agreement. The woman Helen knew was called Patsy was competing with Harry to get a word in.

"Did you think it could be coins and things?"

"I don't know, I could do with a valuable find."

"A hum." Helen had crept up behind the group, they jumped.

"You were saying?"

"Umm, sorry we didn't know you were behind us." Said Patsy.

"Don't worry, I'm not here to judge you. Can you tell me where Tom is?"

"Sure, he went back to his car, over there." Replied Harry.

Helen walked towards the gate and down the lane towards his land rover near the road. There was the group of friends, they were drinking coffee and eating their sandwiches. It would have been great to go to her boot and grab a coffee, but she had a job to do.

"Tom?"

"Yes, umm sorry I can't remember your name." replied Tom.

"I'm PC Helen Johnson. Can I ask you to come with me, my gov wants a word, he wants to know who owns this land?"

"Sure thing." He put his sandwich back in the lunch box. "Now you be a good girl Bella I won't be long." Tom tickled his dog under her ears and she laid down as if she understood what he had said.

"She's well behaved, Tom."

"She has to be, I can't keep running after her, I need to know where she is so she doesn't get under a tractor wheel, mind you if she saw a hare, she would be off like a rocket. Mr Gray wouldn't let me search on his land if I didn't respect his wishes."

"Is that the land owner?"

"Yes, a really nice guy."

They walked back to Robert and Karen. They were almost half way down the track when they heard a loud whistle. Helen turned back toward the car park and saw Kevin the forensic officer holding up a bag and shouting something.

"I won't be a moment; I better see what he wants. You carry on and can you let the gov know the forensic officer is here."

"No problem." He carried on towards the officers.

"Why, PC Johnson we meet again, no body this time?"

"Not yet Kevin." She laughed. "Do you need a hand?"

"That's why I called you back, can't have you empty handed. Here." He handed Helen a case. Kevin tried to wheel his trolly along the track but gave up and carried it after nearly losing it a couple times. He was around 45-50 a bit grumpy at times and had a very sharp eye for details. He was greying on the sides of his hairline which was also reseeding slightly. When they caught up with Tom, he was giving Karen details of the farm owner and contact details, she thanked him then asked him if he would mind returning to the group for now. Robert thanked him and said they wouldn't be long.

Kevin opened his case and removed a forensic suit.

"So, Helen can you tell me what we have?"

"The detecting group found the large coffin shapes vessel and were scraping away the earth when myself and Karen headed over to them to see what they were doing. When we realised what they had uncovered we asked them to move away and not to touch anything."

"So how deep is this vessel?"

"I'm not sure it is still in the ground and we haven't touched it, but it doesn't seem very deep as we could see the bottom and I would say it's around 30cm at the most."

"And what did you find?"

"It seems to have a lot of watches, cameras, phones and some jewellery."

"Well hopefully this won't take too long. Now Helen, you will assist me until the others arrive, as my lad is not well today and you called me away from my lunch, the rest of my team should be here will in about 30 minutes."

Kevin didn't hang around he continued towards the evidence.

"Move back." He was waving his hand at Karen and Robert.

"Helen has told me what you have found now we will find the rest."

"What do you mean?" asked Robert. Kevin pulled on his suit.

"Didn't you think it's a bit shallow? I mean if that is the bottom it would be easy to lift it up." Kevin held onto the side and attempted to lift it; it didn't budge.

Robert went to try and Kevin slapped his hand. "Gloves"

"Yes, sorry." When he had donned on his gloves, he too, tried to lift it, with no success.

"So, what do you think Kevin?"

"Well, if I'm right. Ah ha." He had moved the goods to one side in the corner and was pointing at a screw head. "Pass me a Philips screw driver Helen."

She opened his case and recovered one.

"Right can you bag all this trash and label it then we can see if there is anything below this lid."

Karen and Robert grabbed some evidence bags and emptied it as quickly as they could. He got to work removing the screws. There was 12 in all.

"Well, whatever is under this, was not meant to be disturbed. Give us a hand Robert."

They together carefully lifted it. As they removed it the smell was the first thing that caught them, then the sight. There was a man's body. He looked like he had been trying to get out.

"Well, what do we have here? Helen, can you get my Dictaphone, it's in the side pocket. Stand back I will take a quick look then go into more details." Helen handed it to him and stepped back.

"We have a male Caucasian around 30ish, I would say has been here no longer than 6 months well preserved due to the air tight container and from the expression on his face I would say he was buried alive."

"Oh my god." gasped Karen.

"Less of the dramatics girl. You should have got used to it by now." Kevin continued searching the body. He removed some scraps of paper that looked as thou it had been thrown in with him. The body was dressed in running gear and nice trainers. He obviously enjoyed exercise and spent money on the right gear. The trainers had been worn well but fairly clean, there was dried mud and clay. "Pass me an evidence bag." He was clicking his fingers but not taking his eyes off the trainer.

"Found something?" asked Robert.

"I will know more when I get back to the lab, but this may be very helpful in finding out where he had been."

 Kevin took hold of the victims' hands. There was evidence of torn skin.

"Let's see what is on the underside of the lid."

Kevin and Robert carefully turned the lid over, there was scratch marks and the word SORRY written in what looked like blood.

"Do you think this could have been a punishment killing?" asked Robert.

"Well, the fact that he has written the word sorry says it all. He must have done something wrong and someone has made him pay."

"True, but what? First thing is to find out who he was."

"Gov, there is writing on these pieces of paper." Karen was holding up the evidence bag.

"When we get back to the station you can piece it together, are you any good at jigsaws?"

"I'm not bad at them." She was grinning. Kevin continued to examine the body and surrounding's in the makeshift coffin. The track suit was soiled which suggested he had been in there for a while before he died. He didn't have a watch on and Kevin could just about tell he had been married as there was signs of a ring. His running outfit was expensive.

"I would guess he may have been exercising when he was put in here." Said Kevin.

"But how would you persuade a fit man to get in here?"

"I was getting to that, if you look here and here" Kevin was pointing out areas on the body that had discoloration.

"What are we looking at?" asked Robert.

"This bruising will probably show an area where he has had a drug injected into him, ah there, look." Kevin was directing them to a small almost invisible mark in the bruising around the victim's wrist.

"Wow, you have eagle eyes." Said Helen.

"You better believe it, now you lot get out of the way and leave me to do my job. I will phone you when I have finished."

"It looks like your team has arrived." Said Helen.

"ABOUT BLOODY TIME." He bellowed.

"Ok, it's time we spoke to the others and then we can get back to start sorting what we have." They all headed off to the car park. Robert divided the group up, and they started to take statements.

Helen approached Patsy and Harry. They had run out of steam, competing with each other for attention.

"I won't keep you long I just need your details and may need to ask you to come down to the station later so we can get a full picture of what you may have noticed. So, Patsy how long have you known Harry?"

"What!" Patsy was laughing, "I only met Harry today." She was laughing but seemed a little nervous.

"Yea, we never met till today." Said Harry.

"Oh, I thought you were an item. My apologies." Helen was still convinced on what she saw, their behaviour and the body language. She made a mental note to check it out.

"Can you tell me where you were when the item was found?"

"I was the one that detected it first, does that mean I get a claim on the treasures?" said Harry

"Unfortunately, it isn't that kind of treasure. It is possibly stolen goods; There may be a reward if there is anything of great value but on first glance, I wouldn't think there is anything. I can't tell you more. Well, that's all for now we will see you at the station later."

She left them to join Robert, then turned back. "Someone will phone you with a time, thank-you." She continued towards Robert who was just finishing up, he was speaking with Tom and his wife Clare, getting more details of the farmer and the agreement they had about finder's fee's. Karen was taking the details from the remaining, informing them they would need to come to the station so they could interview everyone in more detail. They were then allowed to go home. The plan was to remove the public from the crime scene as soon as possible so as to prevent contamination of the site.

It was necessary to catalogue all the details however small and this was better done at the station.

"Right, Karen can you return to the station and start on your jigsaw. Helen and I are going to the local farmer, oh and can you start building a list of all the people here and any detail's we may need."

"Yes gov."

They headed back to the cars. Robert put Mr Gray's name and address into the sat nav and then they set off towards his home.

## Chapter 2

On arriving at the farm yard, they passed the manor house and a pair of farm cottages.

"Do you think it's one of them? gov."

"Not according to this, it is directing us up this lane."

 They continued pass the dryer on the right and around the bend up the hill and there in front of them was a red bricked house. It was in need of updating but it looked clean and tidy from the outside. As they got out of the car a middle-aged woman came out of the side door, followed by an old black Labrador.

"If you're selling anything don't bother, we don't buy from doorstep sellers."

Robert removed his badge and held it up.

"I'm DCI Robert Downton and this is my officer, PC Helen Johnson. Who am I addressing?"

"Oh, sorry love, I'm Mr Gray's housekeeper. I'm afraid he isn't here. He is probably checking on the metal detecting group."

"He's not there, we have just come from them."

"Oh dear, what have they been up to?"

"Nothing." Replied Helen.

"We just need to speak with Mr Gray, can you phone him please. It is important."

"Yes, sure but it will depend where on the farm he is to weather he receives it. The signal is hit and miss." She headed back to the house. "Come on, I expect you could do with a cupper."

Robert and Helen followed her in. It was a cosy kitchen, they had a rayburn which was lit and a large pine table in the centre of the floor. There was a vinyl cloth over and it looked like his housekeeper was making a crumble. Robert loved a juicy apple and blackberry crumble.

At that moment his stomach grumbled.

"Sounds like someone's hungry, good job I made this here sponge." She removed a tea towel from a large chocolate sponge.

Robert was drooling at the sight.

"That would be lovely, Mrs? sorry I didn't get your name."

"Nora, dear I have worked for Mr Gray for years."

"Do you live in?" asked Helen.

"No dear my Sam wouldn't be too happy about that. We live in a tied cottage just down the road."

"Does Sam work on the farm?" asked Robert.

"Yes dear, all his working life and his father before him. Sit yourself down." Nora went to put the kettle on.

"Sorry to rush you but could you try to contact Mr Gray it is important."

"Of course, he is probably on his way back, he always seems to know when I put the kettle on. I swear he can smell it."

This made Helen smile, it was the thing her mother always used to say about her dad. It was nice to think about her parents even though they were both gone now, and it still hurt. They never got to meet their granddaughter. She could still remember the day she got the news. Helen was having a 6-month scan and was supposed to be meeting her parents for lunch at 1pm in a little coffee shop near the Queen mother statue in Poundbury. She had waited till 2pm and that is when she had a call informing her, they had died in a head on crash with an articulated lorry. She was told they died instantly and wouldn't have known anything about it. Helen thought she was going to lose the baby because of all the distress she was feeling. Thankfully she managed to go full term.

"Do you take sugar?" Dora was addressing Helen.

"Sorry, no thank-you."

"That's ok. Now is there anything I can help you with while we wait."

"What do you know about the metal detecting group?" asked Robert.

"Nothing really, I just heard they were going to be walking all over No man's land."

"Is that what the field is called?" asked Helen.

"Yes dear."

"Why are the fields named?" asked Robert.

"Well, all the fields have different names that go back generations. How else would they know where to go when Mr Gray needs a field to be ploughed?  Can't very well say I need you to plough the field up the track by the road then follow the other track second one on your right. No, it's quicker to say the name of the field then we all know what he means."

"Ah, and these are passed down to each farmer?"

"As I said generations."

 "Anyway, has they been any strangers around that area, say in the last year?"

"Umm, not really. Only the fibre cables been laid up across the field down towards the next village. But they didn't disturb much, they have them their mole things."

"Ah, yes, I know what you mean, which internet provider was it?" asked Helen.

"You will have to ask Mr Gray; I can never remember names. That sounds like his truck. Told you he could smell the kettle." Nora busied herself making a drink for him.

"Whose car is parked outside, Nora?" said Mr Gray as he opened the inner door and walked into his kitchen.

Robert arose from his seat put out his hand and said "DCI Robert Downton and this is PC Helen Johnson, are you Mr Gray?"

"Yes, what's this about?"

"Were sorry to trouble you, but we have an incident on your land, I believe you call it no man's land?"

"Incident, that's where the metal detector group is. What the hell have they done?"

"It's not what they have done, it's what they have found." Replied Helen.

"Found!"

"Yes, Mr Gray, they discovered a body."

The room went quiet, they were in shock.

"Who, what do you mean?"

"They detected it and dug it up." Said Helen

"What Helen means is they discovered a metal vessel and when they had excavated it there was a body inside."

"Oh, dear me." Said Nora.

"Nora, are you ok?" asked Mr Gray. "Come and sit down." He took her arm and led her to a chair.

"I'm ok, don't you go fussing. It's just a shock."

"How did it get into my field. Are you saying the body was buried in a metal box or something?"

"Yes sir." Replied Helen.

"Is it male or female?"

"We can't discuss details at this stage but when the body has been removed, I would like you to come with me up to the area and tell me if anything looks different than it should be."

"Do you think it has just been put there, as I was up there two nights ago. I put up signs for Tom to direct his lot where to park and it looked the same as always."

"We think it's been there for at least 6 months." Said Robert.

"Sir can you tell me the last time anyone was working on that field?"

"That's easy, it has been months because the internet cables were laid in October, just after we ploughed. It would have been very disruptive to plant crops while they were laying their cables. So, I told them if they wanted to lay cable across my land, then it had to be after the harvest."

"Can you give me the company details so we can speak with them."

"Sure." He went to a draw over in the corner and removed a letter, handing it to Robert.

"Thank-you. Would they have disturbed the ground much?" asked Helen.

"Not really they had a mole machine that leaves very little evidence that anyone had been there."

"Ok, that's all for now sir, but can I ask you not to go up there until I call you. It shouldn't be too long."

He was happy to agree and Robert and Helen left them in peace to digest what was happening. Robert had left them his card in case they had any questions.

"Well, that was interesting."

"Yes, I think our next place to visit is this." Robert looked at the letter. "Internet connections. Underneath the heading it said "we plan your internet to give you the best experience of your life." That's a strange thing to say."

"It does seem a weird thing to write, oh well it takes all sorts."

They got into the car and headed towards Poole.

"Should we ring ahead gov?"

"I suppose it wouldn't hurt." Using his hands free he phoned to alert them he was on his way."

DCI Robert Downton had moved down to Dorset from Oxford when he was a PC. He had been on a case with DCI Ian White and the DCI put Robert forward to do the training. While on his first case Robert had met Sam Parker and a relationship developed. When he had become a DCI his first case turned into a multiple murder and kidnaping. While working this case he had built up a great team. There was PC Helen Johnson, PC Karen Broad and a new addition was PC Alan Day whom had been sent from London, when he arrived, he thought he knew it all. He was cocky and a bit arrogant, but soon realised what a great team he was working with and once he took on board Robert's advice, he became a real asset in the case of two missing women.

The office in Poole was on the trading estate and set in a cul-de-sac.

"Very smart, must be making good money." Said Helen.

"Yes, but then again, they have to give a good impression. Come on let's see what we can find out about the work they did on the farm."

In the office there was a young woman manning the front desk. Her name tag read Miss Julia Bellows, she was somewhere around 25 and dressed in a smart skirt with a blouse and matching jacket. As they approached the desk Julia looked up from her computer and smiled at them.

"Good afternoon, how can I help you? My name is Julia Bellows."

Helen removed her warrant card and presented it to her.

"I'm PC Helen Johnson and this is DCI Robert Downton. We hope you can help us."

"Yes, of course if I can."

"We would like to know about the job carried out crossing Mr Gray's land 3 miles from Puddletown."

Julia's attention was peaked, she became a little agitated and fidgeted with her hair.

"Well, I will have to speak to the boss, I will see if he's free." She picked up her phone and dialled.

"Mr Maloney, there is a detective here to see you. Yes, yes sir I will show them in." She came out from behind her desk.

"This way." Julia led them through the corridor on their left and tapped on the next door.

"Come-in."

"We'll take it from here." Robert walked pass Julia and walked into Mr Maloney's office.

She tried to hang around but Robert closed the door on her. Mr Maloney was well dressed, clean shaven dark haired neatly cut. He was a good-looking guy. He was looking directly at Helen but she was having none of it.

"Mr Maloney, we would like to know about a job that was carried out by your company."

"Yes, of course, where to?"

Robert gave him the name of the farmer and the farm. He was looking through some programs on his desk top computer.

"Here we go, yes it was 8 months ago. We were laying fibre cable across his field to join up the next village. Hang on I will load the map so you can see exactly where we laid it." He clicked away on the keyboard. "Here we go, can I ask what's this all about?"

"There has been a discovery in the field and we are investigating any one that has been in that field. Can you give me a list of everyone on that job?" asked Robert.

"Sure thing, I can give you their contact numbers to if you like or I can tell you where they are working today."

"How many are there on the team?"

"There is six and they always work in the same team. That way the customers get to know them while they are in a certain area. It is good customer service. Now this was the blue team led by Jack. Mind you Jack left the company after that job."

"Do you know why?"

"His fiancé said they were setting up a new business and he needed to focus all his time on it."

"Strange, did jack come and see you?"

"No, he sent a text briefly out lining he had an opportunity for a great new business."

"Did say what it was?"

"No, he never replied."

"Was that in character?"

"I suppose, he was quite excitable."

"Can I have Jack's details also It would be good to have a list and we would like to visit their work site to see what they do."

"Sure thing."

"Do you know the name of Jack's fiancé?"

"No, but one of the team will know as they often went out together at weekends."

"Thanks, we will visit them and get the info."

"I will phone the group to let them know you're coming now; they are working here." He pointed at the map. "And I will print off the map showing where we laid the cable on Mr Gray's farm."

"Thank-you Mr Maloney, that was my next request. I will need to talk to the team?" replied Robert.

They collected the printouts and headed back to the car. He photographed them and forwarded it to the station so the team could start building information to add to the list of people that had been at the site.

There was Jack Sounds team leader then there was Colin Pain, Eddie Macintosh, Peter Bond, Derek Mantel and Tom Mansfield.

"Do you think the blue team might be able to help us with any details?"

"Never know, they may have noticed something. It won't hurt to gather as much info as possible. You know if anything it will help with a timeline in that area."

Back at the station Karen was doing her jigsaw, after forensic had taken prints off the pieces.  There were a few missing. She had placed the pieces on a cellophane sheet and when she had finished, she placed another piece on top. She then clipped them together to prevent any extra contamination. It read.

*Meet me in the usual place*

*I have something v*

*Important to tell y*

# $\mathcal{K}$

From the note Karen assumed the missing words were very and you but wasn't sure about K, it could be Kate, Karen or Kathrine. Then again it could be Ken, Kevin or Kale.

When Robert got into the car, he phoned the station.

"PC Alan Day, how can I help?"

"Alan, it's DCI Robert Downton can you transfer this call to my office and ask Karen to join you?"

"Yes gov."

"First of all, how's the jigsaw going Karen?"

"Well. gov, there was a few pieces missing but I got the majority of it. It read Meet me in the usual place I have something v important to tell y and then the letter K. I assume the missing words were very and you, but not sure on K?"

"Well done, well you got my list of the team. They were known as the blue team and usually there was 6 in a team but 2 have left. What was their names Helen?"

"There was Jack Sound and Tom Mansfield."

"Hang on isn't that the guy running the course?" said Karen.

"Yes, you are right Karen." Replied Robert. "He never mentioned he had worked for the internet company."

"To be fair gov he didn't know we were looking in that direction." Said Helen.

"Ok, Alan and Karen, I want you to go and speak to Tom and find out as much as you can about when he worked for the blue team and his reasons for leaving. We will find out as much as we can from the remaining 4. Can you also get someone to see if they can find out about Jack Sound and where we might find him?"

"Yes gov."

He finished the call and continued their journey towards a village called Wonston.

It didn't take them long to find the team as the vans were lined up in the centre of the village. There was two men unloading equipment.

"Shall we start with these two?" said Robert.

They locked the car and headed towards the men.

"Afternoon guys, I'm DCI Robert Downton and this is my colleague PC Helen Johnson. May we have a few moments of your time?"

"Sure thing, Mr Maloney phoned us to say you were coming over."

"You are?" asked Helen.

"Colin Pain and this is Eddie Macintosh."

"What do you want to know?" asked Eddie.

"Eddie if you wouldn't mind speaking with me away from Colin. It's just we get a better response when we have chats separate."

"Sure, no problem." Eddie followed Robert over to the car. Eddie was around 25, he was athletically built and covered in tattoos.

"So, Eddie how long have you worked for this company?"

"Well, it's got to be 8 years now, yes 8 years."

"Is Mr Maloney good to work for?"

"Yes, he's fair."

"I see that two of your original team have left since you laid the cable on Mr Gray's farm near Puddletown."

"Yes, Jack. He was our team leader, he left two weeks after we finished and then there was a young guy? What was his name? I know, Tom, he didn't last long."

"How long did Jack work with you guys?"

"He was the team leader for around 7 years."

"So, you must know him well."

"I like to think I did why?"

"No reason we are just building a picture and time line."

"Ok."

"And do you know where he went after he left the company?"

"No, he left on a cloud."

"What do you mean?"

"Well, he told Mr Maloney he was starting a new business but he wouldn't tell anyone what it was. Anyway, a couple of weeks after he left my Ella tells me that Jack's fiancée had told her Jack had buggered off with the wedding fund. It was £15,000."

"What was her name?"

"Susie."

"Do you know her last name?"

"You know I never asked but maybe Ella would know."

"How long did you know Susie?"

"Jack brought her to the club on night around 6 months before he left. He introduced her as his fiancée straight away which was a shock to all of us as we didn't even know he was seeing anyone seriously."

"Do you think he was a loner, someone who kept his life private?"

Eddie started to laugh. "No way he was a devil with the ladies and flirted outrageously with my misses and all the others too."

"So, you socialized with Jack outside of work."

"Yes, what has he done?"

"Nothing that we are aware off. We need to speak with everyone that was near the farm around 6 months ago. We have some possibly stolen goods that were buried in the field close to where you laid the cable, so we are building a timeline."

"Well, it wouldn't be exactly where the cable is as we bury it a minimum of 39inch when we use the mole."

"That's very helpful, of course it could have been buried after you finished."

"I see!"

"Would it be ok to visit your wife. She might be able to help us track down Susie and then find Jack."

"Sure, but she's not my wife we live together but we're not married. Have you a piece of paper, I will write down the details."

"Sorry, one other thing where was the club you use to go to?"

"Wimborne, I will write the address on the other side."

"Thanks again. Could you direct me towards the other guys that worked with Jack? Peter and Derek."

"Yes, they are in the manor house grounds over there." He was pointing over Robert's shoulder.

Meanwhile Helen was speaking to Colin, he was in his early 50s bold carrying a few extra pounds. She asked him how long he had worked for the internet company and how long he had known Jack.

"I've known him for years we worked together in the biscuit factory when he had just left school. He was put on a different shift than me and then I heard he had left to get married. He moved away from the area and then low and behold he turned up as my team leader."

"So, did you ask him about his wife?"

"Oh yes, he made a joke and said she was history. I assumed he got divorced."

Helen jotted down the information.

"What kind of man is he?" Colin was smiling.

"He loves the ladies; he could charm the birds from the tree's"

Colin was smiling.

"Do you have any idea where he might be now?"

"No, I tried phoning him for weeks after he buggered off with Susie's money. He's probably laying low."

"Who's Susie?"

"She was Jack's fiancé; he ran off with her savings."

"Where can I find her?"

"She keeps herself to herself but my wife Ruth might know. Do you want me to phone her?"

"No, I would rather go and see her, she might be able to give me more details to where I might find Jack. I assume she knows Jack."

"Sure, she does, we all use to go out together at the weekends. Ruth will be at work at the moment but she finishes around 4pm." He took out a note book and jotted down Ruth's details. Then tore the page and handed it to her.

"Here you go."

Helen put it in her book and then in her pocket.

"Can I ask, what Jack has done?"

"I don't know if he has done anything but we discovered some goods that are possibly stolen in the field where your team was laying cable. Do you remember anyone hanging around the area?"

"No, not that I can think of."

"Ok. Thank-you for your help. I will be in touch with Ruth."

Helen headed towards the car and saw Robert walking through some gates to a large property. She headed towards him.

"Robert, how did it go?"

"Well, we need to find Jack. He is quite the lady's man. And I think our next step is to visit Eddie's partner she may now where his fiancé is."

"Yes, and Colin's wife to."

"Well let's see what else we can get from the remaining two workers."

They were told very much the same and Peter's wife Lisa and Derek's wife Pauline

both knew Jack's fiancé well. They took all
the details and headed back to the station.

# Chapter 3

Meanwhile Alan and Karen headed out to Tom's address. They lived in a semi-detached cottage on the outskirts of Dorchester. It was an older building with beautiful architecture. There was a long driveway to the cottage and a brick out building on the left. What finished the look was the thatched roof. It looked like it was in need of replacing.

"Do you think they are renting or buying?"

"Don't know but it needs some work. At least they have space for storing the equipment." They parked alongside Tom's truck; the dog started to bark.

"It's ok I've met the dog she's a cutie, very friendly."

"I'm not afraid of a dog." Alan seemed a bit defensive.

"Hey I was only joking, don't be so touchy." She soft punched his shoulder, Karen laughed. The door opened and Tom greeted them.

"Come in, Clare has just put the kettle on."

"Great I'm parched, this is PC Alan Day we just need to ask you a few questions."

"Sure thing, sit yourself down."

The kitchen was cosy, with solid wood units, flagstone floor and cream worktops.

"Your kitchen is really nice Clare." Said Karen.

"Thank-you, it's the only room we have done so far."

"Well, if you do the remaining as well as this you will have a beautiful home."

"Mr Mansfield, can I ask how you came into running these classes?"

"Well, I only started a few months ago. I always loved searching for relics when I was a kid. I use to dig up my parent's garden, mind you I only found dinky toys and Lego."

"What did you do before this job?" asked Karen.

"I worked for an internet cable company."

"What company was that?"

"It's the same one that laid the cable on the farm where we were this morning."

"Why didn't you mention this?" asked Karen.

"To be fair I didn't think it was important."

"And was it because you worked in that field that you chose to take the group there?"

"Well sort of, you see while working for the internet company I gathered a list of the land we worked on as I thought that it could be useful in my new venture."

"So why did you leave?"

"While working for them I would find different things and the guys said they found lots of goodies. It reminded me how I felt when I was a kid and one day, I was chatting to Jack the team leader and he said if you're not happy here, why not set up your own business metal detecting. I laughed at first but it got to thinking it wasn't a bad idea. I saved a few quid and went to the bank and they thought my idea was a good investment, so I took out a small loan to buy some equipment and set up business."

"So how well did you get on with the team at the internet company?"

"Ok, they were a close-knit group and wanted me and Clare to come out with them at weekends to the club but there was something about the way Jack looked at women that I didn't like so I made excuses."

"Would you like to elaborate on that?"

"Well, Jack had asked me to join them on a weekend and to bring Clare. Anyway, luckily Clare had a shift so I went on my own. When I arrived, Jack was leading an older woman onto the dance floor, it was Ruth, he pulled her close to him and danced. I thought she must know him well to be so intimate."

"True."

"Anyway, after two tracks they went to the table to sit down, Ruth sat next to her husband, Colin and Jack sat the other side of Ruth. He slightly turned his back on Ruth but had his right hand under the table. He was chatting to Derek and as I had only just arrived, I was just watching and waiting to join in with the conversation. I looked at Ruth and she went rigid for a split second. When I looked at Jack, he had a smile on his face listening to whatever Derek was saying but he was moving his hand backwards and forward, you know like he was rubbing his leg."

"So, do you think he was touching up Ruth?"

"The way she looked, as if she was a rabbit in the headlights. Yes."

"I made my mind up there and then that I wasn't going to introduce Clare to him."

"Do you see any of the team now you have left?"

"No, but I did see Colin about a fortnight after I left and he told me that Jack had buggered off with Susie's wedding funds."

"Who's Susie?"

"She was Jack's fiancé."

"Blimey." Alan was shocked. "No wonder you said you didn't trust him with girls. You have a good instinct."

"If you don't mind me asking, how do you afford your mortgage with your business being so new?" asked Karen.

"I don't mind at all; I inherited this house from my grandad. He was in a care home for the last 18 months but luckily had enough savings to cover the cost so Dad didn't have to sell it. I was shocked he left it to me, I thought he would have left it to Dad." Tom was thinking about the time he came to see grandad when he was a boy and they would go fishing in the stream behind the house. It was such wonderful memories. He never caught very much, just Dog fish and water fleas.

"Darling, darling." Clare was talking to Tom.

"Sorry, I was thinking about grandad."

"Well. That's all for now. Thank you for your cooperation. We will be on our way.

## Chapter 4

When Robert returned to the station, he gathered the team together and also commandeered trainee PC Jess Holt and PC John Wood.

"Right let's get everyone up to date. Would you do the honours Helen."

"Ok, we have a male body that looks like was buried alive and the ME thinks he was injected so the murderer could get him in the tin coffin. Have we had any news from Kevin?"

"Not yet Helen." Replied John.

"Have you got the list of items found with the victim?"

"Yes, here." Jess handed the print out to Her.

"That's your job Jess to find out as much as you can. I would start with the phones. See if you can find out who they belonged to."

Jess had a big smile on her face and nodded, this was what she loved to do. Researching cross-referencing and she was pretty good at it. She took the list and started to head towards her desk.

Robert interrupted "Not yet guy's you need to hear all the details we have discovered first."

"Sorry."

"That's ok, continue Helen."

"Gov, we spoke to the blue team, that was the team that laid the fibre cable around the time the body was put in the ground." She was addressing Jess and John. "There was 6 in the team and we spoke to 4 of them.  Alan and Karen spoke to Tom who use to work for the internet company. Yes, the same Tom that ran the metal detecting class. Anyway, the 6th member is the team leader and he is called Jack Sound. We haven't found out where to find him yet. Did you have any luck?"

"Not really, but Tom seems to think the team wives might know something if not then Susie Jack's fiancé."

"Do we know her last name?"

"Not yet."

"The guys all said that they use to go out together at weekends with the partners." Said Robert.

"Yes, about that, according to Tom he seemed to think Jack was playing around with at least one of the wives."

"Carry on." Robert's attention perked.

Alan repeated the tale of the club and how Tom thought Jack was groping Ruth under the table. with her husband sat the other side of her. Tom said Jack was grinning. It sounded like he thought of it as a game.

"That would make sense as he is supposed to have run of with Susie's wedding fund."

"£15,000"

"Wow that's a lot." Said Karen.

"It is expensive getting married." Said John.

"Oh yes, how do you know John." Jess asked with a grin.

"I'm getting married next year, so far, my other half has spent £8,000 and that's just the venue. We still have food, photography and her dress."

"Yes, let's get back to the case. I think after what Tom has just told us that Helen and Karen should visit the women, so we will catch up after their interviews but now let's call it a night after we have added the blue team's names to our board."

Chapter 5

Helen and Karen decided to visit Ruth first as Tom had described her as a little timid and more likely to open up about Jack with a bit of gentle persuasion.

"I will start by asking about Susie and where to find her. Then you can speak about Jack, see if she will open up."

Karen agreed and they tapped on her door.

"Coming." They could hear a man's voice.

"Oh no, we need to speak to her on her own." Said Helen.

"Don't worry I know how to get rid of him." Karen was smiling.

Colin opened the door with a big smile.

"Come in ladies." He stood to one side to let them in. They nodded and walked in. they saw Ruth sat on the sofa looking nervous.

"Hello Ruth I'm PC Helen Johnston and this is my colleague PC Karen Board."

"Do you think you could make us a cuppa, Colin? While we have a chat with Ruth. You know girl talk. This could be a long one, especially when we talk about you men." Laughed Karen. This made Colin a little uncomfortable. Karen then added.

"You don't mind us talking about woman's problems and sex and things."

"Why would you need to talk about things like that? I thought you just needed to know where Susie was."

"We do but I thought it would be good to find out about Jack and Susie's relationship."

"I would love to stay but I have a job to do." He grabbed his coat and keys and was out the door before Karen could add anything else.

"Would you like me to make some tea?" asked Ruth.

"That's ok, we just thought it's easier to chat without the men around, hope you don't mind." Said Helen.

Ruth was twisting a cloth in her hands.

"Hey don't fret. You're not in any trouble."

"Sorry, it's just that I have never had anything to do with the police."

"We are just trying to find Jack, Colin said you might be able to direct us to Susie."

"I saw her last week in town, she's getting on with her life at last."

"Do you know where we can find her? Have you a contact number?"

"Yes, hang on I'll get it." Ruth went to her handbag to retrieve her phone.

She was around 48, very shy, quite attractive. Slightly overweight but with womanly curves. Looking around her home it was obvious the age group that lived here. They had pictures of holidays, a dog and what Helen thought was parents of Ruth or Colin.

"Have you any children?" asked Karen.

"Um no we were never blessed."

"I'm sorry, I didn't mean to upset you."

"No, you haven't. We came to terms with it years ago."

"Anyway, the number."

"Here, I don't know where she lives."

"Don't worry." Said Helen.

"What did you think about Jack?" asked Karen.

"What do you mean?"

"How would you describe him?"

"I don't know I mean he is fit. He exercised a lot. He took care of his appearance. I don't know what else you need to know."

"I believe you all went out on weekends to a club."

"Yes."

"So, there was music drinking and was there food?"

"Yes, it was a good evening."

"Did Colin like dancing?"

"Oh god no, he was happy having a drink and scampi and chips. He always said he had two left feet."

"So, you didn't get to dance much?"

"Not a lot but sometimes someone would ask me and Colin didn't mind."

"Did you ever dance with Jack?"

Ruth shifted in her seat, she started to grip her jumper and twisted in her fingers. Karen stayed quiet, waiting. She knew not speaking would unnerve her.

"Yes, I danced with him once. All the women danced with Jack he liked the ladies and loved to be the centre of attention."

"What was he like as a dancer?"

"What do you mean?"

"Did he hold you close or at arm's length."

"Arm's length." She was quite sharp with her reply.

"Are you sure about that Ruth?"

"What do you mean?"

"We were told he held you very close and had wondering hands." Ruth burst into tears. Helen put her arm around her.

"Karen, can you make a cup of tea for Ruth."

"Sure thing." She left the room and Helen gently coax her into talking.

"Why are you so upset Ruth."

"If Colin found out." She burst into tears again.

"Tell me about it." She waited for Ruth to compose herself then she told them about the shock she felt when he gripped her ass.

"I didn't do anything as I thought he was drunk and didn't want to bring attention to myself." She paused then continued. "But when I went back to the table, he gripped my inner thigh and I froze, I didn't know what to do, I felt foolish."

"Why should you feel foolish, he was wrong not you. Did it stop there?"

"I…………I'm ashamed to say no. He turned up on my doorstep on the following Monday saying he was in the area and needed the loo. I let him in and offered him a coffee." She stopped for a while and Karen brought her a cup of tea.

"Thank you, you must think I'm a terrible woman. How could I be so stupid. I should have thrown him out straight away."

"We're not here to judge you Ruth, just tell us what happened."

"I'm too embarrassed." She put her head into her hands.

"Hey, don't, he used you."

Ruth told them of that day when she was seduced by Jack and how he kept coming back saying if she tried to stop this, he would feel compelled to tell Colin as he wouldn't be able to live with it."

"So, he was basically blackmailing you."

"I had never thought of it like that. You're right."

"It must have been hard for you to see Susie knowing Jack was cheating on her."

"Yes, but Susie knows now. I told her what he was like, after he ran off."

"Well, you were very brave."

"Please don't tell my husband, please."

"We won't be doing that. For now, we need to speak to Susie. We will leave you in peace and thank you for being so brave Ruth."

"One more thing, do you think Jack could have been doing the same to other women?" asked Karen.

"I don't know, but I wouldn't be surprised."

"He seemed to get off on the hold he had on you." Said Helen.

"How did Susie take the news?"

"She was angry with me to start with then she calmed down and realised there was signs he was hiding something. We stopped going to the club after Jack disappeared."

"Ok that's all for now, thank-you."

In the car Helen phoned the number they had been given. Susie didn't answer so she left a message asking her to contact them as soon as she received this message.

"Now we wait for her call, I think the next visit should be Ella, agree?"

"Should we phone first to make sure she's home?"

"Good plan." She was home so they arranged to come over straight away.

"So, what do we know about Ella and Eddie."

"Eddie is around mid-30s, I don't know anything about Ella except she works and Eddie referred her as his partner so they are not married."

The address was in the new Poundbury, the house was overlooked by properties. There was a small flower boarder along the front of the house and a gate to the left which led to the rear of the property.

They locked the car doors and headed to the front door. The door opened and a young girl no more than 22 or 23 asked them to come in. She seemed in a hurry.

"Sorry, it's just we have such nosey neighbours."

"Hi, are you Ella?" asked Helen.

"Yes."

"I'm PC Helen Johnson and this is PC Karen Board. "

"Please sit yourself down, you wanted to know where Susie is?" Helen put her hand up to stop her speaking. "Yes. But we would like to ask you a few things first. What can you tell me about Susie and Jack's relationship?"

Ella was taken back she was a bit annoyed from being cut short.

"All I know is they were engaged and Susie really loved him, not that he deserved her."

"Why do you say that?"

"He was a terrible flirt and I wouldn't put it passed him to cheat on her."

"So did you mention it to Susie."

"Good god no, it would have killed her. I mean she saw him through rose tinted glasses. He could talk the talk and twist everything to his advantage."

"Would you like to elaborate?"

Susie went a shade of pink; she rose up and stood facing out the window.

"He, tried it on with me and when I confronted him, he said I had given him the signals and that he felt so bad that he said he would tell my Colin all about it." She was almost whispering. Helen didn't say anything she knew Ella had more to say.

"I begged him not to say anything and...............he said he wouldn't if I made it worth, his while."

"What did he want?" Helen was talking softly so as to coax her to continue.

"He started saying he only wanted a kiss." She sobbed into her hands, then continued.

"But it didn't stop there, I didn't know what to do."

"It's ok I get the picture." Helen looked across at Karen. "We really need to find this peace of scum."

"I agree."

"I think that's all for now Ella. Please don't worry we won't let Colin know. That is up to you to decide, if he needs to know. We have Susie's contact number; do you know where she lives?"

"No, she moved after Jack disappeared."

"Ok, we will leave it there; we will show ourselves out."

Back in the car Helen phoned Robert to inform him of their findings. He agreed they really had to find Jack quickly.

"Right, we will see what we can find out about Jacks first marriage." Said Robert.

"That's if he was married?"

"True, we don't know what to believe with this man."

"Do you girls want to carry on speaking to the other women. See if he messed with any of them."

"God, do you think he could off?" said Karen.

"I wouldn't put it past him." Replied Helen. "We need the details on where Derek and Pauline live and." She referred to her notes Peter and Lisa live."

"We'll send it to you, keep me posted."

"Will do. Have you heard from Kevin about who the body is?"

"Not yet, I'm about to go over to see him, so I might be out of signal for a while." Robert cut the call; it wasn't long before the text with the addresses came through.

"We need to speak to Susie too."

Helen phoned her number again, this time she answered. "Hello, is this Susie?"

"Who wants to know?" she sounded very flat.

"This is PC Helen Johnston from Dorchester police station. We have been trying to contact you."

"How do I know you are who you say you are?"

"Your right to be wary, if you would like to phone the station and ask for me then you can confirm I am who I say I am."

"Ok." She cut the call.

Around 10 minutes later a call was put through to Helen and she arranged for Susie to come in to speak to her. She would be around an hour or so as she lived in Bournemouth. This gave them time to visit Pauline and Lisa.

As it happened, they both had been manipulated by Jack and all 4 women when asked do you think he was having an affair with anyone else, replied they wouldn't put it past him but they didn't know.

Karen and Helen knew they had to find out what Susie knew and if she knew about the others. But most of all where they could find Jack.

"I would like to concentrate on this thread. Alan, could you find out as much as you can on Jack's wife. Jess and John, can you gather information on the people that were at the metal detecting site, or and you can leave Helen and Karen off your list."

They looked at the girls, and then realised Robert was grinning.

"We need answers. Come on team let's get this done."

Chapter 6

When Susie arrived, she was shown to the interview room. Helen and Karen looked through the two-way mirror.

"She looks very calm." Said Helen.

"I'm surprised she didn't ask what this was about."

"Yes, come on let's get started."

Helen was to lead the interview and Karen

Was to observe her reactions.

"First of all, can I ask you your full name?"

"Susie Elizabeth Sky."

"Thank-you for coming in today, I expect you are wondering why we need to speak to you."

"I assume you're trying to find out where Jacks gone. Ruth told me you were looking for him. What's he done now?"

"Ah I see, so why didn't you contact us when she told you?"

"She phoned me just after I put the phone down on you."

"Ok, well yes, we do need to know about Jack. Can you tell me about him?"

"There's not much to say, we were engaged and he ran off with the wedding funds. End of story."

"Have you seen him recently?"

"No, I haven't seen him since he ran off with my money and I don't want to see him again."

"Ok, can we go back to when you first met him, tell me about him."

"Why are you so interested in Jack?"

"Can you please answer our questions."

Susie was agitated and fiddling with her clothes.

"I was a temp at his work place the first time I saw him. He tried to get me on a date but I was in a relationship at the time. Then about 18 months ago. I covered 3 days. He used his charms and secured a date for the following weekend."

"Where did he live?"

"I don't know I never asked and he never told me. It wasn't until we got engaged that he asked if he could move in with me. He said we are getting married so why wait. At the time I was besotted with him and agreed with everything he said."

She started to cough a little.

"Would you like a glass of water Susie?" asked Karen.

"Yes please."

Karen left to get a glass.

"Are you ok to continue?" asked Helen.

"Yes, anyway we got engaged 2 months after we met. I thought he was the one. He made me feel I was the most important girl in the world."

Karen came back in. After she had a sip, they continued.

"How did you feel when you found out he had been cheating on you?"

Susie looked shocked, she acted as if see didn't believe Helen.

"I don't know what you're talking about."

"Come on Susie, Ruth told you."

"Yes." She was quiet for a moment. "She saw me in Poole one afternoon and broke down saying she was so sorry. I mean she wanted my forgiveness when she was cheating on her husband with my fiancé."

"So, you didn't know he was playing away?"

"No! I didn't. "

"What did you say to Ruth?"

"I was angry to start with, then she told me how it started and I recognised the pattern and knew Ruth was caught in a catch 22."

"So, were there any others?"

"What, wasn't 1 enough. No not that I was aware off but then I didn't know about Ruth so he could have been at it all the time."

"You had no knowledge at all?"

"No!"

"Ok, let's move on."

"Why do you want to find him?"

Helen wondered how long it would take her to ask that question.

"We are talking to the whole of the blue team from the internet company about an ongoing case." Susie looked a bit confused.

"Case, what case?"

"I can't say at the moment. Can you tell me, did Jack have any hobbies?"

"Hobbies?"

"Yes, what did he like to do when he wasn't working?"

"I don't know what you mean."

"Did he go to the gym?"

"No, he loved to run, He was training for a race or so he told me. I don't know what to believe about him anymore."

"I can understand that. So, he was quite fit, was he?"

"Yes."

"Did Jack have a car?"

"Why do you want to know?"

"Well, we could find out where he is if we can track his car. We can contact the DVLA."

"No, I drove and he used the works van."

"Did Jack ever talk about his family; you know where he was from?"

"No."

"Did Jack speak about his first wife?"

"He didn't have a wife; he was never married."

"That's strange, Colin has known Jack for years and said Jack left the biscuit factory to get married and when he returned to work for the internet company, he told him that she was history."

Susie was quiet for a moment; she was battling with her emotions.

"That can't be right."

"Well, let's move on. Did you ever visit any of the sites that Jack worked on?"

"Sometimes, I would bring him lunch if it was local to our home."

"And where was that?"

"We rented a flat in Poole."

"Is that where you are now?"

"No, I moved when he disappeared. I didn't want him finding me after he took my wedding fund."

"Karen, do you have anything you need to ask Susie?" asked Helen.

"I can see Jack has really hurt you, we are not trying to upset you. We are trying to follow up any leads on people that may have been close to our ongoing case."

"I get that, but if I don't know about the case. How do I know if I've been close to your case?"

"We just need to know the sites you may have been to that the blue team have worked on."

"I have to think, I have been to several. Um can I let you know. I have a diary at home and it may jog my memory."

"That's fine, maybe you can bring it in with you." Said Helen.

"If you could bring it tomorrow that would be great." Said Karen.

"It's private."

"We understand, we don't need to read it but it would help us with dates and times."

"What date did Jack disappear?" asked Helen.

"It was the last weekend in October."

"And what happened on that day?"

"I told you, he ran off with my money. I remember he said he was going for a run and would be back in the afternoon. I told him I was working till 6pm so would see him later. I left the same time as him and that was the last time, I saw him. I was going on my hen weekend that night so was annoyed he wasn't home to say goodbye. It wasn't till the next day when I hadn't heard from him that I got suspicions. When I got home, I went to our saving tin and I found it empty."

"Why did you think he would have taken the money? Couldn't he of had an accident."

"If you had met him, you would have understood, he was always going to the tin and counting it. He was obsessing with it. When I asked him why he was always checking on it, he said it excited him to think we were a step closer to getting married. Like I said he knew what to say."

"Well, we will leave it for now." Helen rose from her seat and shook Susie's hand. Susie was physically shaking at the thought of Jack and the way he had treated her. Jess escorted her out.

## Chapter 7

When Robert arrived at the coroner's office, he found Kevin washing up.

"Great timing, Robert."

Robert was siding up to the body, he was fascinated to see Kevin's handy work.

"Don't touch anything."

"I wasn't going to."

"You might be surprised at what we found."

"What's he got? the dreaded lurgy?"

"He had aids."

"What!" Robert stepped back. "I never thought about that. Could you catch it even after he has been dead?"

"I don't think so but I'm not going to take any chances. We took samples for DNA and bloods. That's when it showed up."

"How far advanced was it?"

"Let's just say he knew he had it."

"What makes you say that?"

"There was a very small trace of the drugs he would have been taking." He headed to his office and Robert followed.

"So, we have a match for his dental records, his name was Jack Sounds, he was 35 and as I suspected, he was drugged before being put in the tin coffin."

Robert gave a long whistle, "Wow, so it's our missing team leader. Do you know if he was drugged while in the field?"

"I would say, it would make sense as otherwise the person or persons would have to transfer him to the site and that would be more work. but as it was 6-8 months ago, there isn't a lot of evidence left around the area. You might want to find out how he got there as it's not the easiest place to get to."

"What about the items found with him?"

"Clean, but we have a partial print from the film in the camera. I've sent it for development should have them back later."

"Great, I was wondering if someone drove him there."

"Don't forget he was in his running gear; he may have run there and if so, how far had he run and did he leave his car somewhere. Did he own a car?"

"Ok sherlock, I have it for now. Anything else for me?"

"Not at the moment but I will email the complete report when I have finished. We are looking at the makeshift coffin. We found a metal plate on the underside its difficult to read. I will send you a copy so your team can investigate. All I would say is it would have to been made especially or someone who has the skills to convert it."

"What do you mean?"

"It started out as a metal cabinet, then had a false back put on to reduce the inside. But it was also made so could be easily removed when needed."

"Interesting."

"Now leave me to get on." He then gestured for Robert to leave.

Robert was use to this treatment and didn't make a comment on it, he had enough to check on now, he left and headed back to the station.

The team gathered to find out what Robert had discovered.

"We found Jack." He announced.

"Great when can we talk to him."

"There's the problem, he's, our body."

"Bloody hell." Said Alan.

"That's not all, he had Aids. So, the next question is, did Susie know?"

"And what about the other women."

"The bastard, sleeping around knowing he had that. Assuming he knew?" asked Helen.

"Yes, he knew, there was traces of the drugs he would have been taking which means these women are probably infected too."

"How do you want to play this gov?"

"We first need to establish what the women knew. Helen, you and Karen speak to them again. This time have them come to the station."

"Do we let them know we found Jack?"

"Yes, it's time to come clean and see the response. They will need to get tested and their partners as well."

"If they knew about Jack's condition it would give them reason to bump him off." Said Alan.

"But do they know about each other?" asked Karen.

"That's the question, surely it would take more than one person to pull this murder off."

"Yes, I bet Susie knew about his aids." Said Helen.

"Well, let's start with Susie, if we phone her straight away, she won't of got very far. She could be back in half an hour. Alan, would you phone the other women and get them to come down as soon as possible. "

"You want them here at the same time?"

"Yes, and I would like Jess to sit at this desk and observe them. You can pretend to be working on the laptop so they think you are not involved in this case."

"Sure, thing gov."

Thirty minutes later Susie was back in the station, she was pretty annoyed to be called back so quickly.

"Thank-you for coming back, Susie, we wouldn't have called you back if it wasn't important. We have some new evidence that we need to share with you."

"This is ridiculous, I answered your questions. I don't know where he is."

"But we do." Said Karen.

"What!"

"Yes, Susie we have found Jack." Said Helen.

"I don't care about him I don't want to know where he is. You called me back to tell me this. You could have told me over the phone. Really this is a waste of my time."

"Susie, if you could just listen." Karen was watching Susie closely. "Don't you want to get your money back?"

She was a bit taken back, "I, umm, yes I mean I wouldn't think he has it still."

"Well, no he hasn't. He is dead." Said Helen. She waited for a response.

Susie buried her head in her hands and started to sob quietly, was it genuine?

"What happened?" asked Susie.

"He was murdered,"

"What!"

"Murdered, and it was around the same time he disappeared. So, is there anything you might want to tell us?"

"What, no nothing."

"You know we have forensic and it tells us a lot. So, I ask again is there anything you want to tell us?"

She shook her head but never said anything. It was time to tell her of their findings.

"Susie, have you had any medical check-ups in the last 6 months?"

"What do you want to know that for?"

"Well, I would think you would want to know if Jack had given you anything. After all he was sleeping around and not just with Ruth."

Susie glared at Helen. "You think he may have given me an SDI?"

"Or something a lot more deadly."

She looked away. "Ok. Ok," she screamed. "Yes, yes, I found out he must have had Aids. Happy now."

"No, we are not happy, we are sorry to hear he was so reckless. Has he given it to you?" Helen had softened her voice and gave

Susie time to compose herself. She nodded her head and whispered a small "Yes."

"I'm so sorry Susie. How are you coping with it?" asked Karen

"It is being managed well with medication, but that's my love life finished with. No one would want a relationship with me now."

"When did he tell you about his condition?"

"He didn't, I found out after he had left."

"How did that happen?"

"I was having a medical and blood test, that's when it was found. They told me I needed to inform any sexual partners. I told them I was engaged and that Jack was my only sexual partner. That was when they said I needed to speak with Jack."

"Did you try to contact him?"

"No, I was so angry and scared. I couldn't think straight."

"Ok, Susie, I think you need a rest. We will get a drink." They left her to sort a cup of tea.

"What do you think Helen?"

"I'm not sure. If she knew before it would give her a great motive. I mean I think I would want to kill the bastard myself."

When they returned, she seemed a bit more composed.

"Did you tell Ruth about the Aids when she told you about her affair with Jack?"

"No, I'm ashamed to say I didn't, I didn't know how to tell her." She put her head in her hands again. "I know I should have. I'm so sorry."

"Would you have any objections if we confirmed the timing of when you found out you had aids?"

"You think I'm lying?"

"We have to confirm details, and this would save us coming back to this again at a later date."

"You understand, we have to be thorough." Said Helen.

"Ok."

"Thank-you."

"We will leave it there for now. I do appreciate this has been hard for you."

Susie nodded then left the interview room.

Sat in the hallway the four women waiting to speak to the police were catching up.

"What do you think they want to speak to us about?" asked Lisa.

"I don't know, I told them I didn't know where to find Jack." Replied Pauline. Ruth and Ella were very quiet, they sat and listened to the chatter. All the while Jess was tapping away on the keyboard and making notes on their conversation.

"What did you tell the police about Jack's behaviour towards women?" asked Lisa.

"I told them about his flirting and the way he would act suggestive towards us all."

"You said what?" piped up Ella.

"Thanks a lot Pauline." Said Ruth.

"Come on we all saw the way Jack held you very close on the dance floor."

"I didn't want his attention; you know what he was like. He made my skin crawl."

"Yes, we know, but it didn't stop him." Whispered Ella.

At that moment Susie came out of the interview room.

"Susie how are you, it's so good to see you?" they were all talking at once. She was desperate to leave and muttered that she was fine but couldn't stop and chat.

"That was rather rude." Said Lisa. "What's eating her?"

"She didn't want to talk to us." Replied Ella.

"I don't blame her "said Ruth in a very quiet voice. The girls hadn't heard her but Jess did. Ruth felt oddly a lot lighter since she had revealed the affair to the police women. She was about to have her world turned upside down.

"Ruth, would you mind coming in?" asked Helen. "We won't keep you long."

Ruth stood and walked towards the interview room. "See you girls later."

They all looked anxious; the waiting was playing havoc with their imagination. Ella was thinking the police would say they were going to tell Eric about her affair with Jack, how was she going to cope if they did? She was hyperventilating just thinking about it.

Lisa was thinking they wouldn't tell Peter, they had promised so, what the hell did they want with her now? She was quite sure it was just to document her previous chat.

Pauline thought she wished she had never been so stupid in the first place to of gotten involved with Jack. The PCs were probably thinking she was desperate for attention at her age. She thought about the way Jack had flattered her telling her how gorgeous she was and she had lapped it all up, the stupid fool that she was. She had made efforts to look good at all times and had lost a few pounds, but after 6 months she had turned into her shell for protection. She would never be so gullible again.

Pauline was dressed in a buttoned-up top and below the knee skirt. She had very little make-up. The whole look was very under stated. Jess thought she would be a very good-looking woman if she made a little effort.

## Chapter 8

"Please take a seat." Helen gestured for Ruth to sit opposite her. She was nervously looking around the room.

"Please Ruth don't be nervous, we just want to bring you up to date with developments." Said Karen.

"Developments? Have you found Jack?"

"Yes, we have, but it's not good news." Helen was looking at her notes. "I'm afraid he is dead." You could see the relief on Ruth's face. She physically sighed.

"I'm sorry, but it's a relief that he can't come back and ruin my life."

"I'm sorry to say, he may still have ruined your life even after his death."

"What do you mean?"

"Have you had a medical lately?" asked Karen.

She looked at Karen "What do you mean? Why do you ask that?"

"Ruth, you need to get checked for aids."

"What!...............no, no that can't be. He couldn't. could he?" she was rambling. She was shaking her head; she was going into shock. Karen left the room and went for a cup of tea.

"I'm afraid when the medical examiner gave us his findings, he informed us that Jack had full blown aids."

"Maybe he didn't know." Ruth was trying to make excuses for him.

"No, we have been told he knew about this as the meds that he would have been on were still detectable, even after all this time."

"What do you mean all this time? How long has he been dead? Did he die of aids?"

"Take a breath Ruth. No, he didn't die of aids, he was murdered and he has been dead around the same time he disappeared."

"But why would anyone want to murder him. Jack was the life and sole of the party."

"We need you to take a test. If it's positive then you will need to tell Colin."

"Oh god." She broke down in sobs. Karen entered the room and handed Ruth a cup of tea.

"Let it out, it's a lot to take in."

Helen and Karen left her alone. Outside they moved out of earshot.

"I don't think she will give us anything new, do you?" said Helen.

"No, I agree. She needs to process it."

"She didn't ask how he died."

"I don't think we can read much in that, she has the aids bombshell to deal with."

"Right let's speak to Lisa next." They went back into the room and explained that they would leave it there but they would like to know the results of the test and they said they would arrange for a councillor to help her through this ordeal. Ruth was very quiet, as she left the interview room the girls were speaking to her but she was in too much shock to answer them. She just carried on toward the exit.

"Lisa, would you follow me" asked Karen.

 "Is this going to take long?"

"Not too long, but we really need to update you."

Lisa walked into the room and plonked herself down like she was totally bored already. Helen sat opposite and looked through her notes, she thought it would be a good idea to make her sweat a bit. Lisa was acting so cocky.

"Well!"

"One moment Lisa. I have to make a few notes." She jotted down a few things then looked up. "Right, we wanted to bring you up to speed with our findings." She paused then continued. "We have found Jack."

This peaked her attention.

"Where is the bastard."

"In his grave."

"What!.............what do you mean in his grave? What did he die off?"

"He was murdered."

"Murdered!"

"Lisa, can you tell me about the last time you saw Jack."

"You don't think I have anything to do with his murder!"

"No, we are trying to build a time line so we can find out what happened to him."

"You know I haven't seen him since he ran off with Susie's money."

"Can you tell me how far your affair went with Jack?" This took Lisa by surprise. Helen was going for it; she hadn't liked Lisa's attitude.

"I told you this earlier, I don't know why you need me to go over this again."

"We need to know if you exchanged bodily fluids?" asked Karen.

Lisa glared at her. Helen jumped in quickly to defuse the situation.

"I'm sorry we are having to ask you this kind of question, only when the medical examiner had taken samples from Jack, he discovered he had aids." She paused to give Lisa time to digest this.

"I think I'm going to be sick." Said Lisa, she was urging. Karen ran from the room to the staff kitchen. She returned with a roll of kitchen roll. Thankfully she wasn't sick and after a while Lisa was composed again.

"I'm sorry I had to give you such horrendous news."

"Did Susie know?"

"No, it was as much a shock to her as you. She only found out after he had left her. If she was aware of your involvement with Jack, I'm sure she would have told you."

"I wouldn't have thought she would. After all she was going to marry the cheating scum bag."

"Yet you got involved with him."

"I told you, he was blackmailing me. He told me if I finished it, he would feel obliged to speak to Peter."

"Well, you will need to tell him now, as he may be infected as well as yourself."

"Oh god, I hadn't thought about that. He has won hasn't he."

"It depends what you mean won?"

"He must have known he had aids, and he was happy to past it on and I wouldn't put it pass him to be screwing around with other women. Oh my, is that why the other girls are here?"

"Lisa, I think it might be a good idea to get yourself checked out first and then we can talk with you."

She didn't argue and walked out of the interview room.

After going through the same with Pauline they didn't find out a great deal more than they had before the interviews.

# Chapter 9

Robert got the team together to exchange all the details that had been found.

"Right, let's start with Alan, have you been able to discover if Jack was married?"

"Yes, and there is no record of a divorce."

"Do you know who she is?"

"Her name is Florence Sounds and her maidan name was Brown. I haven't been able to find out where she lives yet."

"How long were they married?"

"10 years, she was very young. Only 16 and I searched to see if they had any children and found she had a son 6 months after they married. I can't find the boy's name yet."

"Good work, carry on with that line, we need to speak with her."

"Yes gov."

"So, Jess what have you found out?" Jess went a lovely shade of pink, she lowered her head and shuffled through her notes.

"Jess, look up, I don't bite and we are a team here so if you need help with anything just ask."

"Sorry gov, I looked into the four women. They consisted of Cherrie Black, Teresa watts, Penny Bird and Margret Bent. They each have a bucket list and take it in turns to tick off an item as a group. It was on Cherrie's list to go metal detecting and she informed me that she had found a flyer in her post office advertising a day's experience."

"So, nothing suspicious in their group?"

"No, nothing in my opinion. Sorry I."

"Your opinion is important Jess. Now John what have you found out?" asked Robert.

"I am looking into the group of five. They are Patsy Reed, Laura Backshall, Harry Wood, Mathew Bennet and Trevor Hold. Patsy is 23, she has two jobs. During the day she is a sale's assistant and at weekends she is a barmaid."

"Which bar?" John looked at his notes.

"In a private club near Wimborne."

"Could it be the same one Jack and the team use to go too?" asked Helen.

"Good point, we need to look into that."

"I will find out." Said John.

"Continue."

"Laura joined the group as she knew Clare from school and wanted to support her in their new venture. I haven't found anything else about her yet. Then we have Harry Wood."

"There was something about him I didn't like." Said Helen. "He was a cocky bugger and I still think he knew Patsy."

"He moved to Dorset around a year ago for his job in I T."

"I mean if she worked in the same club that Jack went in then she had a connection, and if I get a picture of Harry, I can ask the staff if they recognise him as a customer that would link him too." Said Helen.

"Great if you think he is suspicious follow your hunch, And the other men?"

"Mathew Bennet is a geek where metal detecting is concerned. He has a website set up where he tells the few followers all about his searches and finds. Then lastly there is Trevor Hold, a quiet guy. I got the impression he was hoping this might be an opportunity to meet someone. When I put in a search it came up with several sites he was registered on. He was looking for a like mind man to share his interest of the outdoors."

"Ok, well for now concentrate on Patsy and Harry, if Helen says she thinks there is a connection, then I bet there is one." Said Robert.

"I hope I'm right." Laughed Helen.

"You often are." Said Karen.

"So, going on what we know so far, the ladies that Jack seduced could all have motives."

"But they say they didn't know about him having aids and I'm inclined to believe them, what did you think Helen?"

"Yes, unless they are well rehearsed. Which could mean they were in it together. By the way gov, do we know who the mobiles belong to?"

"The tec team are working on it. It seems strange that whoever murdered him would put random phones and things in with him. They are also looking to see if there are any pictures saved on the camera."

"It is an older camera with a film. I sent it to be developed." Said John.

"Great,"

"That might give us an idea of who it belonged too." Said Helen.

"Well until we hear from them, we need to continue looking into the three persons of interest. Florence Brown, Harry Wood and Patsy Reed. Alan if you and Helen visit the club that Patsy works in and with any luck it is the same one Jack went to."

"I will give Patsy a call to ask her."

"No, phone the club and ask if Patsy works for them."

"Good thinking, we don't want to alert her that we are looking into her and Harry."

"Precisely. Now Karen can you have a fresh look into Florence, you might find something Alan missed, fresh eyes and all that. No, offence Alan."

" None taken, its team work."

"Too right."

"Will do." Replied Karen.

"Jess, you and John see what you can find out about the remaining items from the box."

 Everyone went to their stations to start the search

Alan contacted the club and found that Patsy did in fact work on the weekends. He told the club manager that he and a colleague would be calling in to have a chat. He requested that they didn't inform the staff. He agreed and said "when you arrive ask for Kevin."

Alan updated the gov and set off with Helen.

"I would suggest we speak with the staff separately, and find out if Harry ever went there."

"You really have got it in for Harry and Patsy."

"I'm pretty sure they knew each other before. What are they hiding?"

"Well hopefully we may get a step closer." They drove for a while in silence.

"Do you think they worked together to get rid of Jack?"

"If they did, why?"

"He may have tried it on with Patsy and if Harry had a thing for her, he may have got jealous."

"No, I think there has to be more to it." Said Helen.

"Well. were here, come on let's gather info."

Helen smiled; she could remember when she first started. She had that buzz as well; she wouldn't burst his bubble. The bar was quiet and dark. As they entered a staff member shouted out "were closed."

"We know, were here to see Kevin." Said Alan.

"Oh, sorry, follow me."

"And who are you?" asked Helen.

"I'm the bar manager Susan Holme and you are?" she was quick witted. Helen liked that about her, she smiled and removed her card.

"PC Helen Johnson. We would like a chat with you."

"I thought you wanted to see the boss?"

"Yes, but we will speak with you first."

"Ok, would you like a coffee?"

"Thank-you, we will sit over there." Helen was walking towards a booth in the corner of the bar that was well lit." She wanted to see Susan's face when she answered their questions. You could tell a lot about a person from their facial expressions.

The club was a large room, as you entered the bar was on your right and on the left was the kitchens. On the far wall there was a small stage set up with a dance floor surrounded by tables and chairs. Susan came over to Helen with a coffee percolator and cups. It smelt wonderful to Helen; she hadn't realised how much she needed a coffee fix.

"Thank-you Susan."

"What's this all about?"

"We are just checking a few leads in our case and would appreciate some help." Said Alan.

"How many staff do you look after Susan?" asked Helen.

"There are 6 on my team including myself."

"And do they work in fixed shifts?"

"Mainly, we have 3 staff on week days and 4 at weekends, when we have live music."

"So, you must work quite a few shifts."

"Yes, I have Sunday and Mondays off. Kevin takes charge of the team on those days. We have to keep a close eye on the running of the bar. You would be surprised how many staff I have had to sack for giving free drinks to their friends."

"I can well believe it. So, the team on the weekend, are they reliable?"

"Yes, we have a great team Tom and Mike are very popular with the ladies and Patsy with the men, but don't get me wrong I mean they know how to handle them without antagonising them. When the customer has had a few drinks, they can be a handful but my team knows how to calm them down without upset."

"That's great, I suppose you have regulars?"

"Yes, and you get to know them well. They are our bread and butter, so to speak."

"So, would you know the guys that worked for an internet company? I hear they came here at weekends."

"Oh, yes Jack and the team. Mind you we haven't seen him in quite a while."

"I'm sorry to inform you Jack 's dead."

"I'm sorry to hear that."

Helen cleared her throat, then continued.

"So...., Jack would chat to you and your team?"

"Yes, he had a thing for Patsy."

"In what way?"

"I don't mean she was involved with him. He would try to chat her up, but she wouldn't have any of that. She could see the way he was with the women he was with. He flirted outrageously."

"So, he thought he was a god's gift to women. So has Patsy a partner?"

"Why do you need to know this?"

"I just thought she might have a guy that looked out for her."

"Well, I don't know if they are involved with each other but there is a guy that comes in and Patsy seems to spend her free time chatting with him."

"Do you know who he is?"

"No. He has only been coming to the club for around 9 months. He always wants to be served by Patsy."

"Can you describe him?"

"He has dark hair shoulder length, slim built and I think brown eyes. Oh, and tattoos on his arms."

"You don't know his name, do you?"

"No, but Patsy would know it."

"Ok, that's a great help. When was the last time you saw him?"

"Last weekend. Why are you so interested in him?"

"We are interested in anyone who may have been in contact with Jack."

"Oh, he never spoke to Jack, in fact he kept himself to himself. The only person he spoke to was Patsy."

"If we got a picture of this man, would you be able to confirm it was him?"

"Sure, but how will you do that if you don't know who he is?"

"Well, I assume your camera's work." Helen was pointing to the camera facing the bar."

"Yes, well thought of. If you follow me, we can go to see Kevin and then you can see the footage."

"Thank-you Susan." They followed her to the manager's office. Kevin was on the phone but he beckoned them in.

"Yes dear, yes, yes, look I have to go I have visitors.  bye love, bye.  Sorry about that you must be PC Johnston and PC Day, please take a seat. Susan, can you get the officers some coffee?"

"Susan has already given us coffee and been very helpful. We would like her to stay with us, she may be able to help us. Can we see the footage on your security cameras for last Saturday?"

"Can I ask why?"

"Boss, you remember I said we haven't seen the guys that worked on the internet company for a while. Well, it turns out Jack is dead."

"But we haven't seen them for ages, why do you need to see footage when he hasn't been here?"

"Let me explain." Alan interrupted, "We believe your barmaid Patsy had spoken to him and we were looking into things and discovered she had a friend whom may have known Jack as well. We think we know this person but need to be sure it is the right guy."

"But if this guy has spoken to Patsy and she had served Jack, what has that to do with this guy?"

"I know it sounds strange, but we have our reason for not going into more detail. Could we look at the footage please."

"Yes, give me a minute." Kevin opened a file and selected the one from Saturday. "Here we are now let's find this fellow." He scrolled through and Susan looked over his shoulder.

"There." She pointed. "Go back a bit there he is. It's not a great picture but it's not too bad."

Kevin turned the screen around and Helen looked at it and then at Alan.

"Could we have a copy of this? It is very useful and we would appreciate it if you kept this to yourselves. Please don't mention this to any other team members. We wouldn't want to upset any one until we are sure of our facts."

"No problem officers we won't tell a sole, but is Patsy in any trouble?" Replied Kevin.

"No, but she may be able to help us."

"You have been very helpful and we appreciate it. We will keep your club out of this and be in touch if we need any further help." Helen got up to leave, she shook

Kevin's hand and Susan. "Thanks again."
They left and headed to the car.

"Well, they both have some explaining to
do." Alan stated.

"They certainly do." She was grinning. "Let's
phone ahead for Robert to get them down
the station."

Helen said she would drive back to the
station while Alan filled Robert in.

On arrival they walked in behind Patsy and
Harry whom were chatting together in
whispers.

"Hello again." Said Helen rather loudly. This
made them jump. Patsy's face dropped as
she realised; they were behind them.

"Officers, I didn't see you. I was just saying
to, umm sorry what was your name?" she
was looking at Harry.

"Harry."

"Oh yes, Harry that we must have been
called in to give our account of the day. Will
there be a reward for finding the missing
bits and pieces?"

"No there won't, but I'm sure you can help us sort out a few things." Said Alan.

"Patsy, can you follow me." Said Helen.

"Sure thing." She turned to Harry and smiled. "Isn't this exciting, I've never given a statement before."

Harry didn't reply he followed through to the waiting area.

"So, where do I start?" asked Patsy all bubbly.

"You can start by telling us about your relationship with Harry?" said Helen.

She was taken back, when she recovered her shock, she quickly replied she didn't have one with him.

"So, this isn't you and Harry chatting in the club where you work." Helen placed a picture of them on the table.

"That's not Harry."

"What about this one and this one." She placed more shots alongside. Patsy went quiet. She didn't look up at Helen.

"Come on Patsy, you better come clean. What are you hiding?"

"Nothing, I only just met him and my boss doesn't like us to get involved with the customers."

"Is that the best you can come up with. So how come we are reliably informed that Harry has been coming to the club for at least 9 months."

"I, I don't know what this has to do with you."

"Well, there is the thing. You said you didn't know Harry; how can I believe anything you tell me." Helen placed a picture of Jack Infront of her. "And do you know this man?" Patsy went a little pale.

"Yes, he is a customer at the club, or at least he was. We haven't seen him for quite a while."

"Can you remember the last time you saw him?"

"I'm not sure, it would be months ago."

"Ok, what can you tell me about this Jack fellow."

"Not much, he was a regular at the club when there was live music and he was always with a large group of people. He liked to be the centre of attention."

"In what way?"

"He liked the ladies and they liked him."

"Did you like him?"

"No."

"Are you sure?"

"Yes, I'm sure. I saw the way he would work on the women and they were daft enough to fall for it."

"So, he wasn't a fan of yours."

"I don't like the way he treated women."

"Ok, so did he ever speak to you, did he tell you, his name?"

"I think he told the bar manager his name, Jack wasn't it."

"Yes, that's right, and when you were serving him did you hear anything about his work or friends?"

"I didn't really listen, I knew he work for an internet company, or so Susan told me and he loved to brag on about how he was in charge of a team of men."

"Brag, in what way?"

"He would say they would do anything for him and so would their partners."

"What did you make of that?"

"I supposed they were into swinging."

"You thought they shared partners?"

"Well, I think Jack did but I'm not sure if the others did."

"So, tell me about Harry."

"There's not much to say. We chat and he is very shy."

"Have you been out on a date with him?"

"No."

"What has Jack done?"

"He's dead."

"What!" she sat staring at Helen not moving her gaze. Either Patsy was a great actor or she knew nothing of Jacks murder. Helen wasn't sure.

"Ok, that will be all for a moment. we will leave you here while we have a chat with Harry." Before Patsy could reply Helen left the room.

Harry had been shown to another interview room and was fidgeting. Helen and Alan entered the room.

"Sorry to keep you, Harry. This shouldn't take long."

"She placed the photo's down in front of Harry.

"I'm not going to waste yours or my time. How long have you been in a relationship with Patsy?"

Harry was looking at the pictures and was getting more and more agitated.

"Well?"

"What's it got to do with you."

"When I asked you if you knew each other you said you had only just met."

"I don't know why it's such a big thing. I like to keep my personal life private."

"That's fine, but if you had just said you knew each other than we wouldn't have looked into you and Patsy and we wouldn't have discovered your connection to our case."

"What you think we stole the Knick knacks we dug up?"

"How long have you been involved with Patsy?"

"Not long. What's it got to do with you?"

"Would you tell us how you two met?"

"I was on holiday and like live music. The lady which owned the B&B told me about the club and I went on that weekend and the rest is history."

"Where do you live and what do you do for a living?"

"Why the interest?"

"Please just answer the question."

"I live in Devon and I work for a building merchant."

"And how come you are here again instead of at work?"

"If you must know I hurt my back and I'm sighed off work. So, I came to visit Patsy. I come up every other weekend. Why the interest?"

"She knew Jack the man who was murdered and we are interviewing everyone that came into contact with him."

"Well. we had nothing to do with him or the stolen goods."

"Well, that remains to be found out. Do you know this man?" Helen placed Jacks picture on the table.

"No."

"Have a closer look."

"I don't think so."

"So, you never saw him at the club?"

"I may have but I'm not sure."

"Ok, I think that is all for now. Thank-you."

"That's it, I had to come in just for that."

"Yes Harry, unless you have anything to add?" said Helen.

"No." he went quiet.  Helen grabbed her notes and left the room.

"I will show you out." Said Alan.

"No need I think I can find my way out." He pushed his chair back and stormed through the door.

When they reached Robert's office Helen opened the door and they entered.

"Well?"

"I don't know, I mean we know now that Harry knew Patsy and she had spoken to Jack. Harry is insisting he may have seen him but hadn't spoken to him."

"Yes, and if we are to believe him, we are no closer." Said Alan.

"So, we are back to the women as our suspects." Said Robert. He went to his office door and called. "Karen any joy with finding the wife."

"I found some of her Facebook friends and I have sent out a friend's request. Just waiting for a response. I have also found out where she was born. Cornwall, and her mother still lives there. I have left a message for her to phone me when she gets back from wherever she has gone."

"Well done, Karen, call me when you hear anything. John, any news on the phones or camera?"

"The sim cards have been removed, but one of the phones had some numbers saved on the phone itself. I have phoned one and it was a dentist. They weren't much help but then I got lucky, the other number was the owner's mother."

"So, you have a name?"

"Yes gov, the woman said hello Ruth, I thought you had lost this phone. I explained that the phone had been found and we were trying to return it to the rightful owner. She said Ruth had reported her phone as stolen to the local police in Dorchester and refused to tell me her last name and where we could find her. She said if you are the police than we should have her details on file."

"So have you been able to match anything?"

"Well, I thought I would go through the records of 6 months ago and couldn't find anything, so I went back another 6 months and then struck lucky. It was Ruth Pain."

"You are joking. One of the wives."

"Yes, so I started to wonder if any of the other wives may have lost their phones and would you believe it, they all had reported their phones been stolen."

"Did it state where they think their phone were stolen from?"

"Oh yes, Wimborne working man's club. The same one that the team would go to at a weekend."

"So, our murderer may have visited the club."

"That's what I thought,"

"That would mean the ladies are not suspects." Said Karen.

"It looks like it, but we won't rule it out. They may want us to think that." Said Alan.

"But the phones have put them in the lime light and wouldn't they want to keep a low profile if they were involved?" said Jess.

"Very true. Karen, when Mrs Brown contacts us I would like to be in on the chat."

"Yes gov."

"Well done team, keep searching." Said Robert.

## Chapter 10

Ruth had sat outside for 2 hours; she was trying to pluck up the courage to go into the clinic. She didn't want anyone to see her. When she went through the doors see was shocked to see Ella sitting in the waiting room. She was about to turn to leave when Ella looked up. She turned a shade of pink.

"Ruth, I, ...........I needed a check-up."

"Ella, you too, did he blackmail you as well?"

"I don't know what you're talking about."

"Come on Ella, Jack was a bastard. He cheated on Susie and flirted with us all, but it didn't stop there. Now we have possibly got aids." She slumped do into her chair bursting into tears.

"Oh, Ruth what have we done. How will I tell Eddie?"

"How will I tell Colin."

They hung on to each other, sobbing. The consulting door opened and out walked Lisa.

"Try not to worry Mrs Bond, we will have your results in a few days."

"Thank-you nurse." She turned to leave then saw the girls.

" Oh my god."

"Lisa, not you as well." Said Ruth.

They all started to cry together.

"Ella. Would you like to come in?" said the nurse. Ella broke away from the girls and followed the nurse through to the consulting room.

"We will wait for you here," said Ruth.

"Yes" said Lisa.

Ella nodded acceptance, she couldn't get words out, she was so scared.

"Do you think Pauline has been affected too?" asked Lisa.

"I wouldn't be surprised. I feel so ashamed."

Lisa held Ruth's hand and sat in silence waiting. When Ella returned to the waiting room Ruth was called in. They said they would be here when she had finished.

Lisa told Ella about their conversation about Pauline.

"I'm going to phone her." Said Ella. "We can't have her trying to deal with this on her own."

"What are you going to say?"

"I will tell her that I have had the test and if you don't mind about you and Ruth. Hopefully she will open up as well."

"Ok, if she does ask her if she can meet us for a coffee. We need to process this together."

Lisa agreed. She managed to get through and sure enough Pauline had been for a blood test as well, she said she was on her way and would meet them in their favourite café.

Ruth came out of the room and joined the girls.

"Come on we all need a cup of tea." Said Lisa. They left their cars in the carpark and walked the short distance to the coffee shop where they had often met. No one was talking they all needed time to mule over the events that had just unfolded. When they arrived, they found Pauline waiting at a corner table with a very long look on her face, she gave a half smile when she saw them.

"I've ordered tea if that's ok?" said Pauline.

"Thanks." Replied Ruth.

"Well, this is awkward." Said Ella.

"Ok, let me start. Jack flattered me and made me very foolish. I had no intention of it going any further but he said if I didn't, he would feel compelled to tell Derek."

"He did the same with me." Piped up Ruth. "I was so stupid; I should have known he was reeling me in."

"Don't you dare. He knew he had Aids and still tried to infect us."

"I wish he was still alive so I could kill him myself." Said Ella.

"We have to wait now to see if he has signed our death warrant."

"It doesn't mean we will die; we can have a cocktail of drugs to keep it under control."

"We may as well be dead, how am I going to tell Eddie?" Ruth burst into tears.

"Come on now, we are in this together. We can talk to our men together if you like."

"Oh, I don't know about that." Said Lisa.

"At least they would see that Jack had blackmailed us all. My Colin would think I had been easily led into it and would blame me."

"I think we need to wait until we get the results." Said Pauline.

"That's a good idea, we can have time to think about how we deal with this."

Ruth was very quiet. "What about Susie? Do we tell her?"

"No, I couldn't. She would never forgive us,"

"She forgave me." Said Ruth. They all looked at her.

"What do you mean, you told her?"

"Yes, but she wasn't surprised he had been cheating on her. When I told her how it started, she recognised the pattern."

"Do you think she knew he had aids?"

"No, I wouldn't have thought so." Said Ruth.

"I don't know, when she left the station, she didn't seem so shocked as we were." Said Lisa.

"Come to think about it, you're right. She didn't want to look at us at all."

"But she didn't know about us, did she?"

"I don't know." Replied Ruth. They drank their tea in silence. It was now a waiting game.

# Chapter 11

The next morning at the station the team were busy checking on information. The photos from the camera had been delivered and Robert was looking through them. He was surprised at what he was looking at. He left his office and went to speak to the team.

"Guy's gather around we have the photos back and they are very interesting." Robert put them on the table.

"Oh my god," said Helen. "I don't believe it."

There in front of them were pictures of the team's wives. Each one was with Jack entering a building. There were also images of Jack with his hands on the women.

"Whoever took these, knew their stuff. There was no chance that the women could say it was Jack just being friendly."

"I agree gov."

"It would mean the women didn't murder him." Said Karen.

"Unless it's a double bluff."

"But this evidence points the finger straight to them."

"True."

"Any joy with the phones?"

"I found out they were stolen as we have crime numbers for them and they were all stolen at the club, like the woman said. They all belonged to the team's wives."

"Well, there you go, the murderer definitely wants us to know about Jacks affairs."

"So, could it be Susie? I mean he was cheating on her and he could have been the one to give her Aids."

"Well, we need to press her a bit more. Helen this time take Jess with you. Go to her work place so you can get a feel for her background."

"Ok, come on Jess this could be fun, we will see if we can rattle her cage."

"Is there any other development's that I should know about Alan?"

"I'm looking into Harry and Patsy's background. It looks like Harry was born in Devon and moved to Cornwall with his parents when he was 9. Then he left school and went straight into a job as a driver for a building merchant."

"Good work, when did he move to Dorset?"

"Well, I haven't found out yet, he is still on the payroll as a driver and on sick leave from his job in Devon. I found out what he was signed off for, it's a bad back."

"Did you think he had a bad back?"

"He seemed ok to me."

"Well, go and grill him on this and I suggest you see if there is any connection with the women or Susie."

"Will do."

"John, have we any reply from Florence's mother?"

"Not yet, I thought I would phone her again."

"Yes, get straight onto it. If she answers get me, I want to speak to her." Said Robert.

"I will gov."

She answered on the third ring.

"Hello, who is this?"

"Good morning, is this Mrs Brown?"

"Who wants to know?"

Robert took the phone from Alan.

"DCI Robert Downton, Mrs Brown we are trying to contact your daughter. Can you help us?" She was taken back by his soothing voice and his direct request.

"Yes, I can. What is this about?"

"We have news on her husband."

"What, that waste of space, she doesn't need to know anything about him. The sooner he is dead the better."

"Your wish has been granted." This stopped her in her tracks.

"What! You are joking. So, the aids got him at last."

"You knew he had aids?"

"Yes." She realised she was saying to much so she shut up.

"Mrs Brown, he didn't die of aids. He was murdered."

"What! Oh my god. How did it happen."

"We can't go into details. We really need to speak to Florence."

"She's on holiday, that's why I have Paul."

"Who is Paul?"

"Flo's boy. She needed a break, he's quite a handful."

"In what way?"

"Paul has a few medical problems as well as aids."

"I'm sorry to hear that, so was he born with aids?"

"Yes, that waste of space gave my beautiful girl aids then buggered off, leaving her pregnant and not a word or a penny."

"He certainly was a bad one. So, where has she gone on holiday?"

"I'm not sure, she went on a driving holiday. She said she would see where the road took her, but she phones me every night."

"Could you phone her now? Oh and I would like her number. Ask her to phone me. It is very important."

"I can't promise she will speak to you."

"If she doesn't than we have no choice but to put out a warrant for her arrest."

"You can't mean that, she hasn't done anything."

"Mrs Brown if your daughter does not cooperate with us, we have no choice."

"Ok, ok I will get her to phone you."

"Thank-you, now that wasn't too hard, was it?" she put the phone down.

"I don't think you made a friend there." Laughed Alan.

"That's for sure. Anyway, carry on researching as much as you can about Mrs

Brown and her daughter." Robert went to his office. "Oh, Alan does Mrs Brown have a husband or any other children?"

"I will look into it."

Helen phoned Susie, she was at work and said she wouldn't be able to speak to them until she finished her shift. Helen wasn't going to except that excuse. They headed to her place of work. Susie had a job in a department store in Bournemouth centre.

"Good morning, ladies can I help you?" asked the smartly dressed woman at the information desk.

"Were looking for Susie Sky."

"Who shall I say is asking?"

"PC Johnson and PC Hold."

"Oh, sorry officers. I will get her immediately. If you would like to take a seat." She set off to the first floor. Helen had seen that the fashion floor was situated there and that was where Susie worked.

"How do you want to handle this?" asked Jess.

"We will go with the flow, if a question comes into your head, go for it. I want to rattle her cage."

Jess couldn't think of a thing at that moment. Her mind was blank, she would look an idiot. Why couldn't she be a under control as Helen.

"Hey, don't stress yourself. If you can't think of anything it doesn't matter. Just being here will unsettle her."

"Thanks." Replied Jess.

Susie was walking towards them and didn't look too pleased.

"Why couldn't this wait till I finished work?"

"We have to work on information straight away. Miss Sky. Is there somewhere private we can talk?" said Helen.

"We can use the manager's office." She didn't wait for a response, just marched towards the office. "This better not take long."

"If you are quick with your answers and tell us, what we need to know you could be back to work in five minutes."

Jess closed the door behind them and stood with her back to the door. Helen settled in a chair facing Susie. She opened her note book and looked through some of her notes.

"Now, Miss Sky. Can I call you Susie?"

"Yes."

"Susie, we wanted to know a bit more about your weekends in the club."

"Why would you need to know about them. They were nothing that interesting."

"If you let us ask the questions it will be quicker. Do you remember the weekend when the wives had their mobiles stolen?"

"Yes."

"Was yours stolen?"

"No."

"Didn't you think it strange that the others were taken and none of the men loss there's?"

"I hadn't thought about it, I just thought it was careless of them to leave them on the table."

"So, were did you keep yours's?"

"I always had mine in my jeans pocket, and it was a good job I did."

"True, can you tell us about that night and when they discovered they were missing."

"Well, it wasn't any different than any other weekend that I can remember. It was about 6-7months ago."

"It was 7 months. If fact 3 weeks before Jack went missing."

"So"

"Continue please."

"There isn't much to say, we were enjoying the live band and everyone was drinking and dancing. I remember, Jack had asked the barmaid to keep the drinks coming. She kept clearing the table of empty glasses and replacing drinks. Anyway, Ruth said she was off to the loo and the others said they were coming too. I headed to the bar to order some food. I think Jack was dancing with one of the regular women that were there and the men were talking with the next table. I remember we always saw them each time we came to watch live music. On that table was a couple in their 60s and were amazing at dancing. They could have gone pro. Everyone loved to watch them." Susie was smiling at the memory.

"So, as far as you can remember no one came close to the table while the women were in the ladies?" said Jess.

"No, as I said the only one other than are group was the bar staff and I never saw them take anything other than glasses. Also, when they realised the phones were missing, they went up to the bar to report it and the bar manager said she would phone the police and do a search of the staff's lockers."

"Why would she do that?" asked Jess.

"Because Lisa said the only person that could have taken them was the barmaid. I think the manager told Lisa she would search straight away, so to calm her."

"Did you see her search?" asked Helen.

"Yes, she said as I hadn't had my phone stolen it might be a good idea for me to witness it before they phoned the police."

"So, she didn't find anything."

"No, and all the police said was they would give us a crime number. Fat lot of good that was."

"So, Susie can you explain how the phones all turned up with Jack's body?"

"What, you can't think Jack stole them. Why would they be with him?"

"We wondered if you could help us with that."

"How can I help? I don't know anything. I don't know what happened to him."

"You must have been very hurt when you discovered Jack had given you Aids?" said Helen.

"I told you I found out after he had gone missing."

"Tell us about when you found he had disappeared." Said Jess.

"It was the weekend of my hen do. Me and the girls had left on a train to Winchester on the Friday evening and when we returned on the Sunday evening, I discovered the wedding fund missing."

"So, you're saying he could have gone Friday Saturday or Sunday. You didn't try to phone him?"

"No, we had a very busy, well packed weekend and the girls took my mobile. They knew I would have been on the phone all the time."

"Do you remember the date of your Hen do?"

"Yes, it was the last weekend in October."

"Ok, thank-you that is very helpful. We will leave it there. As soon as we have anything we will let you know."

"Why would I want to know." She got up from the desk eager to return to work. Jess moved from the door to allow her to leave and they headed out of the store and back to the car.

"What's our next move?" asked Jess.

"Back to the station."

## Chapter 12

Harry wondered when the police would want to speak to him again, he knew they wouldn't leave it alone. They wanted to know more about the relationship with Patsy.

Robert went to see Patsy again; he had more questions; he took Helen with him.

"DCI, haven't I answered enough of your questions? I only knew Jack from being a customer."

"I know Patsy. We would like you to tell us about the night the ladies had their mobiles stolen."

"That was months ago, I can't remember."

"It was 7 months ago. Please just tell me about that night in your own words."

"There's not much to say, they were sat at their usual table and drinking, dancing and getting drunk."

"Who was buying the drinks?"

"Jack said to keep them coming and he would settle at the end of the evening."

"So did he come up to collect them?"

"No, I had to clear their empty glasses and then put more in front of them. They really went for it. I wouldn't be surprised if they had lost them in the toilets or in the carpark."

"Why do you say that?"

"Well, they were popping to the loo every five minutes and I know a couple of them smoked so went outside for a smoke."

"How did you know about the missing phones?"

"The women spoke to my boss and she did a search of the area then took one of the women into our staff room to search our lockers. I mean that's not on, as if we would steal them."

"Was your friend Harry in that night?" asked Helen.

"Now you want to blame him. He was at the bar all night."

"I'm sure he was, can you tell me about how you came to meet Harry."

"He walked into the bar around a year ago. We just hit it off."

"Did he say why he came to your club?"

"He was on holiday and loves live music. He had asked the B&B if they knew of any clubs and she suggested Harry give us a visit. It was lucky that there was a band on."

"And you started chatting?"

"Yes, we hit it off straight away. I thought it would be short lived, but Harry drove to see me every other weekend and stayed in the B&B." Patsy was smiling at the memory.

"So, you never left the bar all night?" Helen was trying to unnerve her and it was working.

"Yes, I went for a comfort break but ask the manager she will tell you Harry never left the bar."

"Your pretty sure of this." Said Robert.

"Yes!" she practically shouted her reply.

"Ok, would you mind asking your manager to come over?"

Patsy stormed off to the office.

"You rattled her cage, Helen."

"I think she's not telling us everything."

"Well let's see if the Manager has the same story."

Patsy was coming over with her and was about to sit down with her.

"We won't be needing you Patsy, thank-you, but we would love a coffee. Milk no sugar. Now Miss Holmes."

"Please call me Susan."

"Thank-you Susan. We would like you to tell us about the evening when a group of your customers had their phones stolen."

"Oh god I remember that night, it was so bad for business. My boss was not happy at all. We couldn't find anything on the cameras as their table was in a blind spot."

"That was convenient."

"For the thief, yes. I took one of the women to our staff room to check our lockers. They seemed happy we weren't involved. That was one thing."

"And did any of your staff leave the bar at any time during the evening?"

"We all had a 5-minute break that night."

"Do you know in which order they went?"

"Yes, we always do the same order. Patsy first. Then me and lastly the relief staff as they don't do a full evening."

"And what time did the women report the theft to you?"

"It would have been around 9.30, yes I know because Patsy was on her break."

Helen looked at Robert, that was an interesting fact. This meant Patsy could have taken the phones and moved them maybe to her car. The question was why would she want to frame the women and possibly murder Jack. It didn't add up, she had to be working with Harry. But why? There wasn't much more they could do for now; they would return to the station and exchange all the information they had gathered.

"You know gov, she answered nearly word for word the same as Harry."

"You think they rehearsed it?"

"Yes."

## Chapter 13

Robert was sorting the timeline of Jack's death. According to Mr Gray, the internet cables were laid in October after the harvest. Susie had her Hen weekend the last weekend in October, so it was possible to say Jack was murdered that weekend. They needed to check when each of the teams last saw him. He went over to Alan.

"What are you working on at the moment?"

"I'm looking into the family history of Mrs Brown. It turns out she was married before and had a child from that marriage. Still checking my details."

"Well can you leave that for a moment and see if you can find out who made the cabinet that was used as a coffin."

"Yes gov."

"You should have the photo of the label from forensics', they found it on the back of the cabinet. It looks like someone scratched as much detail off as they could."

"Don't worry I will try to reconstruct it."

Alan went on to the search engine and typed in office equipment first and came up with suppliers and businesses. Then searched the companies that manufactured metal cabinets. He planned to email the photo to as many companies as he could asking if they recognised the label. Now it was a waiting game.

He went back to the search on Mrs Brown, and found she was married to a Mathew Wood from Manchester, when she was 21. They lived with his parents. The marriage was over 2 years later. Alan then put in a search for Mathew and found he had a criminal record; he had been imprisoned for grievous bodily harm to his wife and baby son and was sentenced to 7 years. but was murdered while in prison when a riot broke out. This is when she moved down to Devon.

So, back to finding out about their child. He found out that she had a boy and he would be 35 years old. The child was Harrison Wood, he now had to find out if he was married and where he lived.

"Alan, can I have a moment?"

"Sure thing gov."

"So, how have you got on?"

"I have sent emails to the manufacture of metal cabinets with a picture of the label. I'm still waiting for a response, meanwhile I went back to the research on Mrs Brown and found she had been married before to a Mathew Wood and they had a son that they named Harrison. He would be around 35 now."

"Hang on, Harrison, that could be Harry his name is Wood and he is around the same age."

"That would give him a motive, if he knew about Jack's aids, he might want to get revenge for his sister and nephew."

"Very true."

"Right team lets gather together. Alan has found something that could change everything." Karen and Helen joined them along with Jess. Robert added the new information to the board, underlining the name <u>Harrison.</u>

"Well, that's a turn up for the books." Said Helen. "I always knew he was a bad one."

"This doesn't prove anything yet, but it does mean he has some answering to do. Karen, can you send a car for him straight away."

"gov."

"Alan, you carry-on finding out all you can on Harry. See if what he has told us tallies up with what you discover. Jess, I need you to take on the search for the cabinet. Alan will fill you in with what he has so far. Helen you and I will have a chat with Harry. We need to find out how he found Jack. Was he working alone? Was his baby sister involved? Karen, you try and contact his sister Florence. We have given her enough time to contact us, if she doesn't cooperate then put out a warrant for her arrest. Find out her feelings about Jack. See how deep her emotions are on this. Do they run deep enough to make her condone murder?"

Karen retrieved the number and punched it in. While she was waiting for an answer, she made a list of leads she would follow if she didn't get a reply.

Raise the warrant for her arrest

Phone Mrs Brown informing her the warrant had been issued.

Insist she came to Dorchester station and if she said she couldn't they would send a car with the blues and two's blaring.

Her thoughts were interrupted by a timid voice.

"Hello. Who is this?"

"Mrs Sound, Mrs Florence Sound this is PC Karen Board, we have been trying to contact you."

"I had to charge my phone, and when it was charged, I saw loads of missed calls. Was it really necessary to scare my mother like that?"

"Mrs Sound I don't think you realise how serious this situation is."

"Don't keep using his name. Call me Flo. Why is it serious, I haven't seen Jack since he left me pregnant and with aids?"

"I understand Flo, where are you at the moment?"

"I'm traveling back towards Dorset, I assumed you want to see me. I should be with you in about 2 hours."

"That's great, well we will wait until you get here to ask you more."

"I really don't know what good I will be, but I will come as soon as I can."

"Thank you, Flo, see you then." Flo didn't reply she just cut her off.

"A bit rude, as well." She headed to see Robert and update him.

"Good, we will keep Harry here so he sees Flo and then watch the sparks fly."

Meanwhile Jess had been following a few new leads in her search for the cabinet. She had noticed it was dented and had what looked like oil marks on the door. She made a call to the forensics department and they confirmed it was diesel and oil mix. So, Jess started to contact some local garages to see if they had changed their workshops lately. She was about to give up when a garage near Wincanton said he hadn't changed his garage but he knew of a garage that had closed around a year ago and there had auctioned off the workshop along with the few cars he had on his forecourt. Jess asked if he had been to the sale and if he could tell him the Auction house that handled it. He gave her the name of the auction house but said he hadn't gone to the sale as he didn't see anything that interested him in the catalogue. Jess thanked him for the information and then got straight onto the auction house. They found the details and emailed the catalogue over to her. She asked when it took place and was told it was 11 months ago. When the email arrived, Jess downloaded the attachment and found there was 480 items listed and no index. Well, this would keep her busy. Half the item's she didn't know what they were but she didn't give up hoping that there would be a cabinet listed. There were some pictures of items and then she saw a cabinet listed. A tin cabinet 6ft high x 3ftwide and 3ft deep. Jess checked the measurements of their make shift coffin and they matched within a few inches.

She decided to speak to the auction house to see if they had any details on this cabinet.

"Good afternoon, Marley Auction house. How can I help you?"

"Good afternoon, I'm PC Jess Hold from Dorchester station. I am hoping you can help me. You sent me your catalogue from a garage sale 11 months ago and there is an item I needed more information on."

"Ok, let me transfer you to Steve Wells, he catalogued the items and may be able to help you."

"Great."

"Hello, Steve Wells, how can I help you."

"We are looking to find out about a cabinet that was used as a coffin and we were wondering if it might be the one in your catalogue for the sale of a garage? Can you describe it to me?"

"I can do better than that I have a picture of it and can send it to you. It was quite a strange item."

"In what way?"

"When you opened the door, it looked like a normal cabinet but there was a false wall and behind that was a space around 12inch deep."

"It sounds like our cabinet, except it's the other way around. When you open the cabinet, it looks shallow then you can remove the back to reveal the remaining depth."

"But that is the same. There are two doors, the owner used it as a wall divider."

"Oh, wow. I'm going to send you a picture of a label. Can you tell me if you recognise it? I don't suppose you know who bought it?"

"Leave it with me, I will see if I can find out her name."

"It was a woman?"

"Yes, she said she wanted it for her father."

"Ok, please let me know when you find out. You have been a great help."

"Hang on, just received your email. Yes, it's the same one."

"How can you be so sure."

"It's defiantly the one, the label is his logo from his garage."

"That's great." Jess was thrilled that she had solved where the cabinet was purchased from. She thanked Steve again then went to find Robert to bring him up to date with her findings.

"Great work Jess, we now know a female is involved. I want you to visit this Steve and take pictures of all the women involved with our investigation. I know we haven't got a picture of Florence but it's unlikely she would have purchased the cabinet."

"I will contact him straight away, to make sure he stays there." Jess headed back to her desk to gather all she needed and contact Steve. This is just the thing that had made her want to join the force. Finding some information and following it up to complete the picture.

When Jess arrived, Steve was waiting for her and suggested they went for coffee. Jess agreed and they left the office heading down the town to a lovely little coffee shop on a side street.

"What coffee would you like Pc Hold?" asked Steve.

"Please call me Jess, cappuccino would be great." He turned to the lady behind the counter and ordered 2 cappuccinos.

"Well Jess what can I help you with?"

"I wondered did you see the woman that purchased the cabinet?"

"Yes, but it was a long time ago."

"If I was to show you a few pictures, would you be able to tell me if any of them were close."

"I will give it a go.

Jess opened her iPad to show him the pictures. First was Susie.

"No.

"What about this one?" she was showing him Patsy.

"No, sorry."

"Don't worry." Jess showed him the remaining women that had known Jack, but again he didn't recognise any of them.

"I think it would be good if you come to the station and work with our team on facial recognition. It really would help us a lot," said Jess.

"Sure, I could come with you now if you like. I would ned a lift back later, if that can be arranged."

"I will bring you back when we have finished. Thank you." She was beaming from ear to ear.

"You should do that more often," said Steve.

"What?"

"Smile, it suits you."

Jess went bright red, she turned to pick up her jacket so as not to let him see how much it had affected her.

"Hey, don't be embarrassed, I didn't mean anything by it. I'm sorry if I upset you."

Jess shook her head, gave a little giggle as to laugh it off.

"It's not that, I always colour up easily. Always have, my mum said it was to do with my hair colour." Jess was a brunette. Steve found her attractive but kept it to himself, he didn't want her to feel uncomfortable.

They headed back to Jess's car and made small talk on the way back to the station. Jess was thinking she shouldn't get so worked up when she coloured up. Many guys had told her it was attractive but whenever she caught sight of herself in a mirror, she thought she looked horrendous.

On arrival Jess took Steve to their profiler. Using his tec he started to build a possible match. Jess left them to it and went to see what Robert would like her to work on next.

"You did a great job finding the cabinet. This will be very helpful in finding the murderer. We are waiting for Florence Sounds to arrive. Would you like to update the white board with your information?"

"Ok gov." Inside Jess was bursting with pride, she had achieved a great deal since joining Roberts team. When she first joined Dorchester police station it seemed she was either on the front desk or making tea for the detectives. All she wanted was to be taken seriously. Now she felt like a real police officer.

When she had finished the update, she went to see how they were getting on with finding a match.

"Any joy?" asked Jess.

"Well, does this look like any of our ladies?" asked Steve.

"Sorry, no but I know this will help. Have you finished?"

The officer nodded and saved the profile.

"I will print this off and then if we find someone close, we can contact you to come back, if that's ok?"

"No problem. I hope this will help."

"Come on, let's get you back." Jess grabbed her keys and Steve followed.

## Chapter 14

Robert went through his notes and went to the whiteboard. Helen joined him. "What you thinking gov?"

"This photo doesn't look like any of the women we have contacted does it."

"No, we can only hope his wife has a resemblance of it."

"True, bet we will still need to find out if she was in the area during the auction. Then we have to find a motive."

"Should we go over all the people that came into contact with Jack?"

Just then Karen joined them.

"I think we should go back to his employment? He must have come into contact with other women and then again could it be a customer that he messed with?"

"Good thinking Karen. While we chat to Florence, I would like you and Alan to visit the internet company. You can chat to the secretary and Alan can talk to the boss man.

I think you will get more from her than if a man is present."

"Ok, we'll keep you up to date." Karen went to Alans work station to inform him of gov's request. On the way Karen read the notes Helen had written on the previous meeting.

"So, the secretary is a Miss Julia Bellow 25 slim, smartly dressed. The manager is a Mr Maloney and is married, middle-aged and was very helpful. Well, it will be interesting to see what we can find out."

"How will you tackle it?"

"I'm not sure I will tell her of Jack's death straight away. I will ask her what she thought of Jack and what she knew of him."

"Do you want me to keep stum about his murder with Mr Maloney?"

"No, you deal with it whichever way you need to. I will tell her once I have gathered as much as I can from her. Let's hope she hasn't heard about it from anyone."

"Yes, hopefully she will still think we are searching for him." Alan parked the car near the entrance and could see a young woman peering through the blinds.

"Do you think that's her?" said Alan.

"She's young and slim. Pretty too."

"If you like that skinny look." Said Alan.

"You don't?"

"No, I like a bit of meat on my woman. Sorry I..." Karen was grinning.

"Don't fret. Come on let's get something to bring back to gov."

They were greeted by Miss Bellow's with her usual greeting.

"Good afternoon I'm Julia Bellow, how can I help you?" she had a wide smile on her face and was looking straight at Alan.

"I would like to see Mr Maloney. Could you tell him PC Alan Day from Dorchester Police station?"

The smile slipped from her face. She nodded and went straight to his office. She tapped lightly on his door.

"Come." Came the reply.

"Mr Maloney, there is a PC Day from Dorchester Police Station wishing to see you."

"Show him in." He was beckoning for her to hurry up.

"Mr Maloney will see you both now."

"That's ok, Miss Bellows I would like to chat to you if that's ok?" said Karen.

"Yes of course. Would you like a coffee?"

"That would be great."

"So, what's this about?"

 "Oh, nothing to worry about we are just building a picture of people that has come into contact with Jack."

"Jack! Still haven't found him. Well, he was quite a bad one with the ladies." Karen didn't jump in with the truth, she just raised her eyebrows as if questioning it.

"Oh?" she waited for Julia to continue as she knew she would.

"Well, I heard he was cheating on his fiancée."

"No."

"Oh yes, mind you he tried it on with me too."

"Tell me more."

"No, I shouldn't."

"Well Julia, I am afraid I must insist you tell me as we need to build up a picture of Jack's last days."

"Last days! What do you mean?"

"I mean we have found Jack, he's dead."

"Oh, really." She went white and slumped down into the nearest chair.

"Just tell me what you know, Julia."

"I, I don't want to." She went back to making the coffee.

"Julia, I have to insist and if you don't talk to me now than we can continue this at the station."

"No, no I will tell you." She handed Karen a coffee and sat at the table in the Kitchen. "It started when Jack joined us, it must have been oh I don't know about 6 years ago. He had the gift of the gab. You know told me I was gorgeous. Brought me in a bunch of flowers saying they were to brighten my day. You know. Anyway, he got me to agree to go out with him. It lasted three dates when I found out I was pregnant."

"How did Jack take that?"

"He didn't, he said I was trying to trap him and he didn't want anything to do with me. He said I must get rid of it. My baby." She burst into tears. Karen let her gather herself. It really was turning out that Jack was determined to ruin as many lives as possible.

"I took a week off and visited a private clinic. Mr Maloney was unaware of what happened as Jack said if I told anyone he would make it his mission to ruin my life. Anyway, when I returned to work, he had moved on to someone else."

"So, you had an abortion."

"No, I let Jack think I had but I continued with the pregnancy. My daughter was born and I had time off to nurse my grandmother. That's what I told everyone."

"How did you hide it?"

"I was lucky as I'm naturally small framed and as it was the summer, I wore loose summer cotton dresses and no one was the wiser."

"So, who looks after your daughter while you work?"

"My mum. We are very close and she knew I couldn't get rid of my baby. It was a good thing to as I can't have any more children."

"Sorry to hear that can you tell me why?"

"I have somehow caught aids and now I won't chance having a relationship with anyone."

"Do you think Jack gave it to you?"

"I don't know."

"So, you had other relationships."

"I did meet a couple of men. But when I found out I had aids." she went quiet. "I stopped dating."

"Did you contact any of the men to ask them to check themselves out?"

"Yes, but I didn't speak to Jack."

"Why?"

"Why should I care if he had it, he probably gave it to me."

"He probably did as we have found out he did have aids."

"Oh my god I should have said something. I might have stopped him passing it on to the other women he messed with. I'm so sorry." She started sobbing again.

"Julia, when did you discover you had aids." "About a year ago."

"What about your daughter, is she ok."

"Thank god she is."

"I'm pleased for you. So, tell me when was the last time you saw Jack?"

"It would have been the day before Susie's hen weekend. He came into the office boasting that he could play away this weekend and did I want to give him another go. I told him I wouldn't touch him with a barge pole. I was tempted as I thought I could give him aids but then I would be a murderer and I couldn't do that to Susie."

"What did you do that weekend?"

"I don't know."

"Come on you remembered he asked you out, surly you can remember."

"It was my baby's birthday and I had a birthday party for her. Yes, that's what I was doing. Why?"

"We believe that was when he was murdered."

"Murdered!"

"Yes, I wonder if you mind if I take a photo of you."

"Why do you want that?"

"It's so we can eliminate you from our enquiry's"

"I don't understand."

"We are taking photos of all the women that have been in contact with Jack. As this is a murder, we have to make sure we check everything. You understand." Karen was banking on Julia not wanting to seem thick. She would want to appear as if she totally understood. Karen knew she could refuse and she had every right to. It worked, she nodded and said she understood it had to be done.

Alan had settled in Mr Maloney's office and was taking notes.

"So can you tell me did you know of Jack's tendency to flirt with other women?"

"Yes, but it was harmless fun. He even tried to flirt with my wife. She had none of it and scolded him for being such a tart." He was laughing at the memory. "Have you found him now, I bet the bugger was shacked up with a new woman."

"Yes, we have found him but, he won't be pestering any other women."

"What do you mean?"

"He's dead. Murdered and that is why we need your help."

"What, I can't believe anyone would murder Jack for flirting."

"I'm afraid it wasn't harmless flirting. He took it further and possibly passed on aids."

Mr Maloney looked shocked, he couldn't answer, he just shook his head and muttered no…. no.

"You can understand why we need to find anyone he got close to."

"Yes, I want to help. He couldn't have known he had it. Poor chap, he would be devastated."

"He knew. He had known since his marriage to Florence and that was some time ago."

"You mean he was married and, what about Susie?  poor girl. Did she know?"

"I can't comment. So, tell me since Jack joined your company how many women is he likely to have been in contact with?"

"Well, only Miss Bellows and a temp while she was off caring for her poorly relative. Come to think about it the temp was Susie."

"His fiancée?"

"Yes, he was a fast worker when it came to women."

"I'm afraid he was. Did he ever mess around with any of the customers?"

"God, I hope not. Do you think he could of?"

"Well going on what we have found out, there is always a chance. Could we have a list of the women he came into contact with, say the last year of his employment."

"Ok, leave it with me and I will get you a list as soon as I can."

"Thank you, Mr Maloney."

"You will be discreet, won't you? This could ruin us if it gets out, we employed someone so reckless with life."

"Don't you worry, we won't mention his condition unless we need to."

"Thanks'."

Alan grabbed his notes and went to catch up with Karen. When they were in the car Alan asked how she got on with Julia. She told him about Jack's baby and how she had kept it from him.

## Chapter 15

Back at the station Robert and Helen went back into the interview room to ask Harry some poignant questions.

"Well, Harry. You haven't been very open with us, have you?" said Robert.

"What do you mean, I've answered all your questions." Replied Harry.

"So, it conveniently slipped your mind that you knew the murdered victim?" said Helen. They were doing the two-prong attack, not giving him too much time to think.

"I told you I didn't know him; I had seen him at the club that's all."

"But that's not true, is it?"

"You forgot to mention that he was your brother-in-law." Robert wasn't going to waste much more time with him, He agreed with Helens first impression there was something about him that didn't run true.

"I don't know what you're talking about."

"We haven't got time for this, Harry we have the facts and your sister is on her way to fill us in with the details." This seemed to rattle his cage. He looked between the pair not knowing what to say next.

"So why didn't you tell us you knew him?"

"Why do you think. I thought you would think I had something to do with his death."

"And you think hiding this from us wouldn't be suspicious?"

"I didn't think." Harry lowered his head, then continued. "I didn't have anything to do with his death, I really did come across him by accident."

"So did you approach him?" asked Helen.

"No, I didn't want anything to do with him after the way he treated Flo."

"Did you tell Florence that you saw Jack?"

"I mentioned it, but she wasn't interested as she put it, she said good luck to him she wanted nothing to do with him."

"Did Jack acknowledge you?"

"No, he didn't know me. I didn't get to Flo's wedding and I only knew what he looked like because she sent me a picture of them on her wedding day."

"So, what did you say to Flo? You don't mind me calling her Flo, do you?"

"No, I don't mind. Well, I told her that I had seen Jack and that he was with some woman that Patsy had told me was his fiancé and I asked her when she got the divorce."

"How did she respond to that news?"

"She said good luck to the cow and no she hadn't got a divorce."

"Ok, we will give it a rest for a moment while we check a few details. We will try not to keep you long."

"I've answered all your questions, can't I go home now?"

"As I said we won't keep you much longer. This will save us calling you back." Robert and Helen left the room. Karen and Alan had just arrived back.

"How did it go?" asked Helen.

"Very interesting." Replied Alan.

"Let's recap on what we know about Jacks movements." He walked to the white board. Helen started the time line.

"We know that Jack married Florence and soon after left her pregnant and arrived in Dorset. He then got a job with the internet company."

"Yes, and then started going out with the Julia Bellows." Added Karen.

"Tell me more?" said Helen.

"He was full on with her and she said when he found out she was pregnant his attitude changed. He told her to get rid of it and said he wasn't interested in her any more. Julia said he said she was a stop gap till something better came along."

"So, she had an abortion?"

"No, she decided to keep the baby and kept it from everyone."

"How the hell did she hide that from Mr Maloney?"

" I asked the same question and she said she was lucky the last stages were during the summer and she wore loose flowing dresses. She said they were the fashion at the time."

"And I assume that would be when Julia went to look after her sick relative. That's what Mr Maloney said." Alan was raising his fingers in averted comer's.

"Yes, Alan and that's when Susie came to work as a temp." replied Karen. "We know that was when Jack first saw Susie."

"Correct, and then who did Jack mess with between first meeting Susie and getting his date with her?" asked Robert.

"Gov, did anyone ask the workers partners how long Jack had been carrying on with them?" asked Alan.

"Good question, Karen could you contact the ladies and find out?"

"Yes gov."

"Let's continue. So, we have discovered that Harry who is Jacks brother-in-law saw Jack in the club and then informed his sister Flo that not only had he seen Jack but that he hadn't realised she had divorced Jack. Anyway, she said she hadn't. Harry said that Flo just said good luck to the women who ever she was as she will need it."

"Do you think she meant it gov?" asked Karen.

"Well, we should be able to find out, she's just arrived. Right Helen let's see what she has to say for herself. Karen, you carry on with speaking to the ladies and Alan see if you can find out what Jack might of got up in the years before he hooked up with Susie. I suggest you speak to the men he worked with."

He went to meet Florence.

 She wasn't what he expected. This sultry looking woman was a stunning woman. 6ft 2in, long blonde hair and she had an air of confidence about her. Robert thought what the hell was wrong with Jack. He had a beautiful wife, yet he couldn't stop playing around.

"Florence, it's nice to meet you, please come this way." Robert headed towards the interview room. Helen followed behind Florence.

"Can I get you a coffee or a tea?" asked Helen.

"A coffee would be great I've been traveling for 3 hours."

"Where have you travelled from?"

"I was traveling down from Yorkshire, and now heading back to my mums to collect my son."

"How come you don't tell your mother where you were?"

"I never know where I'm going to go when I take a holiday, that's the fun of it I drive for days and then when I have travelled 3 days I then head back towards home on a different route."

"So, you don't know where you're going to sleep, I mean you don't plan any accommodation?"

"I don't need any as I sleep in my van."

"What about washing and cooking?"

"I'm not a slob, my van is converted into a mini motorhome. I did it myself. It took me 3 years but now I can go wherever I want."

"Sounds great, you're a dark horse Florence."

"Please call me Flo."

"Flo, can I ask you when did you last see Jack?"

"That would be the day before he left me. I was suffering from morning sickness and I slept in. I never seen him leave so I assumed he didn't come to bed. You see he had a job working at a night club. His hours were long. He said he was saving for a deposit on a house for me and the baby. I had no idea he was saving to leave me with nothing."

"You must have felt really hurt and scared."

"I was for the first week and then I packed up and left to move in with mum. She has been brilliant."

"So, tell me when did you discover you had aids?"

"When I had to have bloods taken during my pregnancy."

"Is there any chance you could have given Jack aids?"

"What! Are you mad? I was a virgin when I met Jack. The bastard gave it to me."

"Ok, I'm sorry but I had to ask. Now can you tell me about the time you heard that Jack was engaged to Susie."

"I don't know what you mean." Flo was looking down at her hands. She didn't look at Robert.

"Come on Flo, we know your brother told you." She was shocked that they had discovered this. What else had they found out?

"I don't know around 18 months ago, what does it matter."

"It matters because Jack was murdered.

"That's nothing to do with me. I didn't care what he did."

"So, you didn't mind the fact that he was spreading aids to other women?"

"I couldn't stop him; it wasn't my responsibility."

"Can you tell me have you been to Dorset before?"

"I've driven through a few times. Why?"

"Didn't you want to see him? To have it out with him. I mean he left you with a child on the way and a dreadful illness."

"I know, but what could I do. Nothing would change that."

"So, you haven't been to see where Jack worked?"

"No, I didn't know where he worked."

Robert was getting nowhere so Helen jumped in.

"Flo, we will need a list of the places and dates you took your holiday breaks for the past 3 years, and any proof that you can provide"

"Is that really necessary?"

"Yes, this is a murder inquiry and we have to check every lead and detail. We will be looking at CTV, traffic cameras and any surveillance footage we can find just to confirm your whereabouts." This seemed to rattle her. She wriggled around in her seat,

"Could I have a comfort break? I've been on the road since 6 this morning."

"Yes, Helen will show you to the ladies and then we will continue." Said Robert. Flo looked a little annoyed that she was going to be chaperoned to the toilet.

"I'm sure I can find my own way there and back." She stood to leave the room.

"I'm sure you can, but the public toilet is out of order so Helen will take you through to the one near the canteen. Oh, and Helen while you are in that area, could you pick up some sandwiches. I expect Flo is peckish. I know I am."

Flo was about to object when her stomach rumbled. She never replied, she just followed without another word.

As they walked along the corridors Helen decided to try another approach.

"Sorry about all that back there. It's my job to get all the facts and check every detail. This must be very hard for you. I mean you have only just heard Jack is dead and you must have loved him once." This softened her. Flo gave a half smile.

"Your right I did love him once, but when he left and I discovered he had given me aids the love turned to hate." She stopped and realising what she had said added. "I mean not enough to kill him. If I had wanted to do that, why wait all these years."

"Maybe because you didn't know where he was."

"If I wanted to find him, I think I could have." She continued walking without another word. While Flo was in the rest room Helen went to pick up some sandwiches and some fresh coffee. They headed back to the interview room.

While the ladies were gone Robert popped in to speak with Harry.

"How much longer is this going to take? I've told you everything I know."

"Nearly done, can you tell me did Flo visit you much?"

"No were not that close, I would see her a special occasion but otherwise we had the odd phone call."

"Did she ever tell you when she was on holiday, I mean didn't she send you messages like wish you were here?"

"Not really, I mean she would sometimes say I will driving through do you want to meet for a coffee."

"Can you remember any of those times?"

"Hang on."

He removed his phone and opened his WhatsApp.

"Here we go." He scrolled down his contacts.

"Can I see?" asked Robert.

"Sure."

Harry passed the phone across.

"Why are you looking at Kitten? Is this her nickname?"

"Yes, she was called Kitten by me when I was little as I struggled with Florence and at that time, she hated being called Flo. It was only after Jack started calling her Kitten that she decides she would prefer to be called Flo."

"Ok, would you mind if I screen shot this? It would save me writing it all out."

"Sure, but I don't see what help this is."

"It will save us a lot of time. There's just one more thing, we need to get our tec team to look at it. We can verify times and places to."

Harry was looking a bit worried, had he just put a spanner in the works. He couldn't refuse now without looking suspicious.

"If you wouldn't mind sitting in the waiting room, hopefully it won't take too long then you are free to go."

Robert left Harry with his phone.

When Robert entered the interview room again, Helen and Flo were sat eating Lunch.

"Hope you've saved me some." He sat down then grabbed his coffee.

"Flo, I wondered if I could see your phone."

"Why?"

"Your phone can give us dates times and locations to save us time waiting for you to list the places you have been recently."

"I don't know, there are private things on there."

"As you said you haven't seen Jack in ages so you have nothing to fear."

"But what if he was in the same area as I was and I didn't know?"

"Then you have nothing to worry about, Harry has happily given us his phone to check his ware abouts," Helen looked at Robert and gave him a knowing look that said well-done great thinking.

Florence removed her phone and gave it to Robert.

"We need your password or number to access it."

"It is fingerprint protected." She took it back unlocked it then handed it back to him.

"Thank-you, if you wish to sit in the waiting room, hopefully it won't take too long."

"How long possibly as I would like to get home before dark."

"I would say 2 hours, so if you wish to go down the town, maybe with your brother. He's in the waiting room."

Flo got up and without waiting went straight to Harry. They embraced and Flo shed a few tears.

"What have you told them?" asked Harry.

"Not here come on were going down town they said they would be finished with our phones in 2 hours."

Harry followed without another word. Robert went to the window to watch them leave. Flo went towards her Van. It was white, with a small chimney out of the roof, but apart from that it didn't look any different than an ordinary van.

"What's so interesting gov?" asked Helen.

"I was just thinking would the cabinet fit in her van?"

"I think it would be a bit tight."

"True but I wonder when she got this van? Let's put it through the system. Maybe we will get lucky."

It turned out she had owned this van for 5 years and when they got the details of the floor space it proved that even with everything taken out the floor space was too short.

"Dam, I thought we might be on to something."

"Gov, it seems Flo was in Dorset around the disappearance of Jack." Said Alan.

"What about when the auction was on?" asked Jess.

"Good thinking Jess." Said Robert.

Alan went back to his search.

"According to her phone roaming she was close to the area. She must have left her phone somewhere as it seems to stay in one place for most of the day."

"Where is it showing?"

"Newport."

"Interesting, so if she left it in Newport could we find out where and see if there is any CCTV that could show her Van. Didn't you say that the auction house said the woman collected the cabinet straight after the auction?"

"Yes, but where did she leave her phone if she had the van and didn't you say the cabinet wouldn't fit in it?"

"I know something isn't right here. Did they say what colour the van was that came to collect the cabinet?"

"I don't have that information; I will phone Steve straight away."

"Steve is it." Said Alan. He was grinning.

"Take no notice of him." Said Karen. Jess ignored him and made the call.

"Afternoon, PC Jess. did you miss me."

This flustered her and she found she was colouring up again. She turned so none of her colleagues could see her face.

"Umm, I forgot to ask you what was the colour of the van that collected the cabinet."

"That's easy it was white, a hire van from Newport. Is there anything else I can do for you?"

"No, that's all thank you unless you know the company's name and number."

"Just a second. Here we are, have you a pen and paper handy."

"Yes."

Steve relayed the name and number and added that they used the company when customers needed large items delivered. Then he said she just as well have his number so if he wasn't at work, she could get hold of him. Jess thanked him and replaced the receiver.

Robert asked Jess to follow up the lead to see if they had any record of the woman and her details.

"I think we could crack this case soon." Said Robert.

"Cross fingers." Said Helen.

## Chapter 16

This was the moment they were not looking forward to. Ruth, Lisa, Pauline and Ella had asked the clinic to give them the results together when they returned. It was safer than being sent to their homes.

"Would you like to come in Ruth." Said the nurse.

"Can my friends come in too?"

"Yes, if you're ok with that."

"I am. Were all in the same boat so just tell me."

"I'm sorry to tell you have aids, but as you have caught it early it can be controlled by medication. You will still be able to have a full and happy life but you need to inform any sexual partners."

Ruth had switched off at "you have aids" how was she going to tell Colin?

"Ruth, are you ok?"

"Yes,"

"Can you get on with it. Put us out of our misery." Said Ella.

"Yes, just tell us please." Said Pauline.

"If, you're sure." They all nodded in agreement.

The nurse informed them all that they were all infected and were in the same situation as Ruth.

The women left the hospital in a daze. They walked to the café on the corner. Ruth ordered tea for them all and joined them.

"What now." Said Lisa. "How are we going to tell them?"

"I think all together."  said Pauline.

"How will this work?" Ella was getting stressed and started to cry.

"Hi come on Ella, we need to keep calm and work out how we are going to approach this."

"I don't know if I can go through with this." Said Ruth.

"We can, I'm going to ask everyone over to mine and we will tell them how Jack blackmailed us all and when they have taken that information in, then we will tell them that he gave us aids. If the worst happens, we will move in together. We can't be alone now." They were all quiet. "Agree."

"Yes." Replied Ella.

"Yes," said Ruth.

"Lisa?" said Pauline. Lisa was very quiet, she whispered yes as well.

This was going to be the worst day of her life thought Ruth, how would Colin respond. She had no idea. He knew that Jack's body had been found but he wasn't aware that Jack had aids.

"Have any of you told them that Jack had aids?" asked Ruth.

"No, I haven't told him anything. He told me he had heard that Jack was found, and that his body had been found at the site where they had worked before Jack went missing."

"Did you wonder who killed him?" asked Ella.

"Well, if my Derek had found out about Jack's blackmailing, he would be first in line." Said Pauline.

"You don't think they found out and done away with him, do you?" asked Ella

"Don't be silly." Answered Pauline, but the thought had crossed her mind. As it had with them all. They drank their tea in silence.

"Come on if they knew we would have known about it. Did anyone notice a different behaviour around the time we went on the hen weekend?" asked Ruth.

Lisa was still very quiet and this concerned Ruth.

"Lisa is everything alright? Your very quiet."

"Yes, it's just that I was thinking Jack disappeared that weekend we went away and we don't know what the men got up to. Come to think about it Susie left us for an hour on that weekend."

"You don't think she could have murdered him, do you?"

"Not on her own."

"So, what are you saying?" asked Pauline.

"Nothing, it's just we don't really know do we." Lisa was planting awful thoughts in their heads. Was Eddie helping Susie. Ella knew he had a soft spot for her and he was very much in favour of helping a damsel in distress.

"Do you think we should tell the police what we know?" asked Lisa.

"No." they all replied.

"We don't want to drop our men in to the police's suspect list. We leave it and ask some discreet questions about that weekend and what they remember of it."

"Good idea, maybe we should hold off telling them about the Aids for a few days." Said Ruth.

"Agree." Said Pauline.

"Yes." Said Ella.

"If, you're sure." Replied Lisa.

So, it was decided to give it a few more days they would then confront it face on.

# Chapter 17

From the phones it showed that Harry was in quite a lot of contact with Flo. Also, it confirmed the time line of when Harry said he had first seen Jack at the club. He had in fact text Flo to inform her that he had just seen Jack.

The response was as followed.

Harry

Hi sis, just seen a ghost. Jack.

Flo

Don't be daft, how much have you been drinking.

Harry

See, I'm not dreaming. He attached a picture taken in club and it was a grainy picture because of the light, but defiantly Jack.

Flo

Oh my god, the bastard. Who's he dancing with?

Harry

His fiancé. You didn't tell me you were divorced.

Flo

 I'm not!!!!!!!!

Harry

Bloody hell, do you want me to tell her?

Flo

No, leave it, I'm not interested. Let the bitch find out the hard way.

Harry

Ok, sis, as long as you are ok.

Flo

X

Harry

Night Kitten.

Flo

Night.

There was a few more comments about 2 months later

Flo

Missed you tonight, called in earlier hoping to have a drink with you.

Harry

why didn't you say you were coming? Where are you now?

Flo

On way home, next time love you.

Strange thing is her phone was reading that she was home all day, so why lie about coming up? Robert continued to compare times and places.

"What do you make of this?" asked Robert.

"She may have written the text and thought she had sent it, and then decided she should let Harry know she had been in the area, just in case someone mentioned her visit." Said Helen.

"But that doesn't make sense. If she had asked after Harry, someone would have mentioned it?"

"I will give the manager a quick call, see if anyone did." Helen went over to her notes to find the contact number.

"When did the ladies get their phones stolen?" asked Robert.

"Here."

 she passed Robert the notes. "Hello, Susan, just the person I wanted to speak to. PC Helen Johnson, here."

Robert left her to her call and went through the dates. It was as he thought. The week before was when the girls had their phones stolen. So, he went back to the notes on Flo's phone. Looking at the roaming information it showed she was in Dorset that week so she could have been in the club that weekend. But it still didn't make sense. Why text Harry the following week informing him that she had been in the area when she hadn't. He made a note to ask her about this when she returned to collect her phone."

"Well?" asked Robert.

"No one asked for Harry that she was aware of."

"You think that's strange, look. She was in the county the weekend when the girls phones were stolen yet she tells Harry through text she called in a week later."

"Strange. Was she in the area around the hen weekend?"

"According to this she hasn't been in this area until today."

"She could have left her phone home and still come to Dorset."

"Yes. I wonder if Jess has found out any more about the hire company.

"She's still working on that. They have to go back through their records."

It was time for Flo and Harry to collect their phones, and right on time they appeared.

"Are you going to question her about that weekend?"

"No, it will keep. We need to collect as much as we can before we alert her to our findings."

"Are our phones ready for us?" asked Flo.

"Yes, I will get them for you." Helen went to collect them." Thank-you for your help. This will save us a lot of man hours and clear this up quicker."

"Good, I need to get home as I'm due to go back to work Monday and need time to settle my lad back at his school."

"Does he go to a local school?"

"It's about 50 miles from my home. They are a special school to cope with his disability's."

"That's got to be expensive?"

"Yes, but I have help and luckily I have a well-paid job."

"What do you do?"

"I'm a legal secretary."

"Very nice." Said Robert.

"I had to get a good job, as I have been bringing my son up on my own."

"Well, you seem to have done well for yourself."

Flo was in no mood to stand there talking about her struggle. She took her phone and turned towards the exit.

"We may need to speak to you again Flo but for now have a safe journey home." said Helen.

Flo didn't reply, just pushed through the door out into the carpark.

"Sorry about my sister, she always has been highly strung."

"Don't worry, thanks again. Hopefully we won't need you again." This put a smile on his face as he took his phone and left heading towards the high street.

"Good idea to let them think we have finished with them. They are more likely to let their guard down."

"Come on let's see how Jess is getting on." Said Robert. "Hope you have some good news for me."

"Yes and no, the hire company said they had hired the van to a garage called Pete's auto. So, I got the contact details and gave them a call. I managed to speak to the owner and he said yes, he remembered the woman. In his words he said.

A lovely quiet spoken brunette, said she was on her way to an auction when she thought her van was making a different sound to what she said it should. She didn't want to get stranded in the middle of nowhere. So, she asked me if I could give it a good going over and if there was any chance, I could give her a curtesy van, so she could pop to the auction house. She told me she would need it all day as if she was going to meet up with an old school mate for lunch. Well, I told her the van sounded ok to me but she insisted I keep it for the day and she would pay me well. I asked him if he got her contact details and would you believe it, she managed to change the subject and distracted him so much that he forgot to take her details. He just let her drive off with the hire van and said see you later. I asked him if he found anything wrong with the van and he said not a thing. In his words it was the easiest money he had earned. She returned around 8pm saying she was so sorry she was late but she got lost as she didn't know the area."

"Didn't he find out any details about her?"

"Only that she hadn't been successful at the auction but had had a lovely lunch with her friend. He had asked her where she came from and she managed to avoid the question."

"Ok so, we still think it could be Flo?"

"Yes, she could easily dye her hair and the details would fit as her phone location was in Newport all day. She must have left it in her van." Said Helen.

"So, we think she used the hire van to collect the cabinet then what?" said Robert.

"Where did she take it?"

"She must have had help, don't you think? I mean it would be awkward to move and very heavy for a woman of her build."

Alan joined them; he had been listening to their discovery.

"Gov, I was thinking as this was some time before the murder of Jack, she would have to store it somewhere."

"Good point."

"Come on guy's think where would you hide a cabinet weeks before you needed it?"

"Close to the site?" said Jess.

"Good."

"Could she have put it in the ground then covered it up waiting for the opportunity to murder him?" said Karen.

"She didn't leave anything to chance, she had this well planned." Robert was pacing the office. "Were missing something. But what?" He went to his office and dialled Kevin's number.

"Kevin, I just wondered was there anything found that couldn't be accounted for?"

"Anything in mind?"

"We have a theory that a woman could be our murderer and we have possibly worked out how she got the cabinet to the site. On a hire van, but can't work out how she could have managed to move it on her own."

"That's easy, sack trucks. There were scratches that would be consistent with the use of them. She could have got it on the sack trucks used the tail gate to lower it off and pushed it to the site. Mind you it wouldn't have been easy the ground was pretty rough."

"Thanks'. I owe you one." Robert joined the others again and told them of Kevin's theory. Now they had to work out how she managed it without anyone seeing.

"I would like you and John to go to the murder site and scout around see if there is any evidence to back our theory's. You

might need wellies we had rain last night."
Alan and John set off.

"While they are gone, we need to work out how Flo got Jack to meet her and see if we can link her to the photos. There are still quite a lot of holes in our case."

"Would you like me to find out when Flo had time off work to come to Dorset?" said Jess.

"Yes, and on that note, I would say it's less likely to be many weekends as if she took the photos Jack wouldn't have visited the women while there was a chance of the men arriving home. I would say he arranged to see them when he knew they were on a job." Said Helen

"I like you're thinking. I will leave it with you girls. Let me know what you come up with." Robert went to his office.

"We need to start from when Flo found out Jack was in Dorset. Let's make a possible timeline.

Harry text Flo informing of Jacks whereabouts.

The end is the murder on the hen weekend."

"We can add the auction date to when she bought the cabinet."

"Did she take the pictures before or after this?"

"I would think before as this was probably what tipped her over."

"True. So do we have any other dates that prove she was in Dorset before the auction date?"

"Hang on." Helen grabbed the list. "She did come to Dorset 4 weeks before."

"Is there anything interesting about that date?"

"Should there be?" asked Karen

"Hang on, wasn't that the day they were finishing the job at Mr Gray's?"

"So, it is. you think Flo could have followed the team to watch Jack."

"Possibly and maybe that's when she got the idea to bury him alive. Think about it, the ground had been ploughed and was easier to dig."

"Mind you it still would have been hard work."

"But that would give her more reason to dig it and bury the cabinet ready for him. Once she had it dug and placed in the hole, she could cover it lightly ready for Jack."

"And as she drugged him that would give her time to uncover the grave put him in and cover him before he came around."

"What an awful way to die."

"That was the idea, she probably thought he had given her and 6 other women a death sentence."

"When you look at it that way."

"Ok if we say she may have dug the hole buried the cabinet and left, when and how did she get the letter luring him to a meet place."

"Also, how would she know about the special place."

Maybe she watched Jack and notice he met the women in a special place. Karen, can you contact the women and ask if they had a special place that they would meet. We need to find it."

"I'll do that straight away." Helen went to see Robert, to tell him their theory's."

"Good work now we need to prove it."

Jess tapped on his door.

"Come in, what have you got for me?"

"I have several dates of when Flo was off sick or took days off during the week." She placed them on his desk.

"Well done, would you put them on the timeline and then we may be able to match them to some events."

## Chapter 18

The journey to her mother's, seemed to take twice as long. The traffic was busy and all this alone time was giving her too much time to think and recall the past 18 months. What was she thinking? She should never have gone to see Jack. He was bad through and through. Harry phoning her that evening telling her that he had seen him, would stay to haunt her. If only she hadn't answered. if only she hadn't asked for proof.

It was done, it wouldn't change the events that followed. Flo pulled into a service station to top up and grab a coffee. In the corner of the shop there was a young couple having a heated conversation.

"You always turn it onto me. You were flirting with her and you make out it's my fault."

"If you don't like it, you know what you can do. It's no skin of my nose."

"Don't be like that. Don't you love me?" she was sobbing quietly, trying not to be noticed.

"As I said if you don't like it, do one." And he walked from the shop out to his beat-up car with the air of "look who I am."

This made Flo's blood boil. She went over to the girl who was trying to console herself.

"Hey, no boy is worth this, I'm sorry but I heard the way he spoke to you and you shouldn't let him get away with it."

The girl quickly turned." It's none of your business." With that she pushed past Flo and stormed after the lad. Flo could see him laughing. He knew exactly what he was doing.

This angered Flo but it wasn't her battle. She paid for her coffee and set off again. Now she was back with her thoughts. She put her music on, trying to distract from going back to that fateful day when she gave in to Jack's advances. She had meant to tell him she would blow his cover and tell Susie he was still married and let her know he had given her aids, if she didn't know it already. Jack being Jack had wormed his way around her.

Flo had been watching Jack at work and was waiting for the right moment to confront him, she had considered speaking to him in front of his colleagues but thought it would backfire, so when he was on his own, she walked over to him. She recalled the conversation.

"I bet you didn't expect to see me again" was her first words. His eye's popped out of his head, she looked amazing. She had made a special effort to let him know what he had lost.

"Wow, you look amazing."

"Keep the remarks to yourself, I haven't come for you. Where is your fiancée?"

"What do you mean, darling?"

"Don't treat me as if I'm stupid."

Jack walked towards Flo and she took a step back. He grinned; she was still wary of him. She realised what he was doing. He was trying to intimidate her like he used to, she stood her ground as he got closer and closer. She mustn't crack. He stopped inches away from her, they were face to face.

"It's good to see you, Kitten."

"Don't call me that, you have no right after you left me."

"Oh yes you were up the duff, hope you got rid of the sprog."

"How dare you, it's none of your business." She wouldn't tell him either way.

He suddenly grabbed her in his arms and kissed her deeply. For a split second she forgot herself and almost gave in to his familiar smell, embrace and God did he know how to kiss a woman. She pushed him away.

"How dare you."

"We are still married darling."

"Not in my eyes, you haven't changed, have you?"

"Well, you can't waste a good thing girl."
This was getting her nowhere. She had to play him at his own game.

"You took me by surprise, what would Susie think if she knew?"

"Why would you want to tell her?"

"Let me think………ahh yes, a little thing like you walking out on me and leaving me a little gift plus aids." She turned to leave, she had to leave him wanting more and wondering if she would kiss and tell, so she glanced over her shoulder in a sultry way then walked out of the trading estate to her van.

Jack couldn't believe how she had changed.

Flo drove out of the estate and as soon as she could pulled into a lay by. She burst into tears. How could he still affect her like that?

She decided to follow him to see what he was up to, but for now she had to head home. A few weeks later Flo was back, she had dyed her hair and pinned it up to throw Jack of the scent if he caught sight of her. She sat waiting for the team to leave their site. keeping a good distance from them she followed, praying she wouldn't be seen, Flo wasn't sure what she was going to see but, in her gut, she thought it would pay off. They arrived at a farm not far from Puddletown. She drove past their vans and parked up out of sight, grabbed her camera and binoculars. As she got a little closer to the guys, she saw Jack go to his van and set off back the way they had come. What was he playing at? she ran back to her car and jumped in, setting off in the same direction as Jack. It wasn't long when he turned off in a different direction. Where was he going? This wasn't towards his store, he turned off down a cull-de-sack and swung into a driveway. She parked the car and got out. She had to try and not look suspicious. Luckily opposite the house was a park with a small wooded area. Flo hid in the thicket and watched.

Jack rang the doorbell and saw a woman answer the door, she seemed surprised to see him. She stepped aside to let him in. Using her zoom lens, she managed to photograph Jack leading the woman up the stairs. She waited in the thicket until she saw Jack leaving and managed to capture another picture of Jack as he gave her a peck on the cheek. She continued to follow Jacks movements for a couple of weeks and she noticed he was visiting other women; it wasn't until she followed him to the club that she realised the women were his work colleagues' partners. Flo couldn't believe it; did they really think she would keep it quiet? She knew she had to think through what her next move was if any.

She left it for a couple of months, but it was eating away at her. Those poor unsuspecting men and his fiancée. It was affecting everything she did. Work mates complained that she was snappy and didn't seem to concentrate, so she decided to take a break and sort this out once and for all. After speaking to Harry, she discovered Susie was having her hen weekend that following Friday night. He had heard them getting all excited about it. Harry said they were going away Friday night and returning Sunday. Flo had pretended she wasn't interested she told Harry if he wants to be caught as a bigamist it was, his problem. But after the chat she realised it was the perfect chance to carry out her plan. Flo had seen an auction on line and found the cabinet which would be perfect for what she had in mind. She realised that the police taking her phone could cause a problem up to the auction date but after that she knew there was no trace as she had left her phone at home. She told her mother she had lost it and was waiting for a replacement. She promised to phone her as soon as she arrived at her destination.

## Chapter 19

Alan and John arrived at the murder scene; they passed the murder site. The edge of the field was the start of a small wooded area. They decided to start in there.

"If I was going to hide a cabinet until I could bury it, I would take it in here." Said Alan.

"But wouldn't she struggle to get in over these brambles and stingers?" replied John.

"Let's see if there is a better area further up the track." They set off. About 20m further there was a track to their left and another one left again which seemed to lead further into the wooded area.

"This looks more promising?"

"Yes, sure does. We need to be very careful not to disturb too much in case we find anything." Said Alan.

There was evidence of a pheasant pen that had been in use a while ago, but didn't look as it was in use now. Behind the remains of a makeshift building was an area that looked as if it had been flattened.

"This could be a possible place she could have hidden the cabinet. Look there is a mark." It looked like a sharp corner indented. John was pointing to an area well hidden from the field.

"I think we need forensics here; they might be able to find something to prove this is where the cabinet was put." He removed his phone and took a picture of John's find and forward it to Robert. Within a minute Robert phoned Alan.

"So, tell me what I'm looking at."

"We found it almost impossible to get through the thicket close to the murder site, so we headed along the track and came across a path that was probably used by a gamekeeper. Anyway, while searching John noticed the sharp indent in the soil and we wondered if she may have stood the cabinet up behind the old building. Should we get forensics here?"

"Yes, I will contact them. You both stay there and direct them to your find. Good work John. Once they have arrived and you have explained what we are looking for, you can return to the station."

"You earnt yourself some brownie points." Said Alan. "That's high praise from the gov."

They retraced their steps and waited for the team to arrive. This time Kevin didn't come out to the site but he sent his assistant Mandy James. She was young but had been working closely with Kevin and was very keen to learn from him. John introduced himself and Alan.

"Great, so what have you for me?" she was beaming as she walked alongside Alan.

"John, do you want to let Mandy know our theory?"

"That's ok. You can do it. Let me carry your kit." She let him take it. Alan was following a few steps behind, so Mandy dropped back into step with him. He explained that they thought a woman had hidden a cabinet somewhere close to the murder site. Alan asked for her opinion.

"What, as a woman?"

"Well, you girls are more logical in your planning and I'm sure you would be able to put a different perspective on it."

"We'll see PC Alan." She was laughing at him.

"Cheeky."

"Sorry, I couldn't resist. You guys are so easily wound up. Anyway, I think you are right if I was to hide something I would make sure it wasn't too close to the site. Let's see what we can find." She walked on and John and Alan waited out on the footpath.

"Give us a call if you find anything, we have to head back to the station." Said Alan.

"Ok." She shouted back.

"She's quite a looker." Said John.

"I hadn't noticed." replied Alan.

"Yea, right. She certainly was interested in you."

"You reckon?"

"She was laughing with you, wasn't she?"

"That doesn't mean anything."

"You're not that funny."

"Cheers mate."

"Come on. Let's get back."

Meanwhile Mandy got on with her search. She instructed the team to looked for prints on the remaining structure, she thought the woman may have put her hands on it to steady herself.

The ground was fairly level, not too bad, but add a heavy cabinet on sack trucks and she would be very lucky if she hadn't slipped a little or loss balance. While they were dusting the building, Mandy was combing the area where John had found the indentation. She took a cast of the area; after photographing, hoping it would match a corner of the cabinet. She then moved some of the vegetation to get to the soil below where she found a trainer print, so took a cast of this as well. It was around a size 6 so possibly belonged to a woman. This seemed to be going well, Mandy was pretty confident this was the hiding place they were looking for. She phoned Alan to let him know her findings so far.

"Your amazing Mandy, think we should go out for a drink to celebrate some time."

This took her by surprise. "Yes, yes that would be nice." She hung up the phone quickly. Nice, why did she say nice? She could have said that would be great, but she said nice.

The other end Alan was thinking why did I say that? What a Dum ass. He looked around to see if anyone had heard him. Luckily it looked like he got away with it.

Robert was looking at what they had now, was it enough to charge Flo with her husband's murder?

They had proof she had bought the cabinet.

They knew she had a higher van to take it to the site.

She knew about his engagement.

They still needed physical evidence of her taking the photo's unless Harry took them.

He went through the report on the items that were discovered with Jack.

They had a partial print on the inside of the camera, so Robert suggested Helen and Karen was to go to Flo's to get her fingerprints and while there, see if they could get some more details from her that might tie in with the chain of events. This meant a journey to Cornwell, hopefully they could get evidence off a woman's trainer to match the print at the site where she may have left the cabinet.

They still needed proof she had met up with Jack. He sent Jess to the industrial estate to ask around the other businesses to see if anyone had seen Flo. She was a stunning woman so would be memorable.

He now had to wait for his team to deliver, hopefully the evidence they needed. He knew they were very close to wrapping up this case.

## Chapter 20

The girls decided they should all meet at the club. Ruth had said safety in numbers.

 "We can ask the men together about their last memories with Jack." Said Ella.

"Good thinking, it can come up in conversation."

Ruth was very nervous on the night and scared that they might slip up and talk about Jack's ways. They arrived at the club, it felt strange. They hadn't been since Jack's disappearance. It wasn't the same the men said, but they had agreed to meet tonight in respect of Jack's memory. Ruth thought they wouldn't be thinking that soon.

Ella, Eddie, Pauline and Derek were sat at their usual table when Ruth and Colin walked in., they had gone to the bar to get a drink.

"I'll get these" said Peter, who just walked in with Lisa.

"Cheers mate. You go join the girls love I will bring your drink across." He said to Ruth.

"Come on Lisa, leave them to sort our drinks." She linked arms with her and headed to the table. As if on cue the men said they were getting another drink and would be back in a minute.

"Now what?" said Pauline.

"We bring up the subject of Jack."

The men returned to the table. Pauline had said she would start the conversation off.

"I couldn't believe Jack was murdered." Said Pauline.

"We know what you're doing girls?" said Peter.

"What do you mean?" asked Lisa, her eyes were darting around the table. She was beginning to panic.

"It's ok, love calm down, I know he was blackmailing you." Said Peter. She turned to look at Peter and burst into tears.

"What do you mean?" said Ruth. She needed to stop Lisa confessing. He couldn't know about Jack, could he?

"Ruth, we know about Jack. Susie told us."

"Oh my god." Pauline was speechless, she looked at the men and then the girls.

"When did you find out?" asked Ella.

"She came back to tell us on the hen weekend." Said Colin.

"Oh no, you didn't murder him, did you?"

"Don't be silly, I wanted to but Susie said it was all in hand. He won't hurt anyone else."

"She didn't, did she? Susie didn't murder him, did she?"

"No. We didn't know what she had planned but she said she wanted us to try and get on with our lives as if we all fell apart then Jack would have ruined even more lives." Said Peter.

"I don't understand, why didn't you mention it to me?" said Ruth.

"We all decided it was better not to speak of this and try to move on."

"But wont the police find out? They will arrest you all."

"No, as Susie said he was already out of the picture before she told us."

"What, murdered?"

"I told you we didn't ask, she said we couldn't get revenge as he wasn't around anymore."

"What do you mean he wasn't around? Had he been murdered?" Eddie was tearing his hair out, they weren't listening.

"She just said that we couldn't get revenge. It was too late."

"I can't take this in.," said Lisa.

"Susie promised she would never mention that she had spoken to us all as long as we kept to our side of the bargain and that was to make things work with you girls." Said Colin. Ruth threw her arms around Colin and hugged him tightly. She suddenly pulled back and with a look of dread said "Did Susie tell you about Jack's illness?"

Colin whispered "Yes." And held onto her tightly.

"Hang on, you mean Susie already knew when I confessed to her?"

"Yes, she knew and that's the reason she cut herself off from everyone. She couldn't trust herself from letting something slip." Said Colin.

"Oh, poor Susie."

"Why let us know now?"

"We knew you had been told by the police about Jack's aids and that you would be having your test."

"But why didn't you mention this before?" said Pauline.

"We didn't want you to carry the burden any longer than you needed to and it wasn't till his body was discovered that we had to face this." Said Peter.

"When did you find out about the aids?"

"Susie told us straight away, she needed us to digest that and realise why Jack was totally to blame."

"So, who killed Jack?"

"We don't know."

They were all quiet, the girls were trying to take it all in. These last few days had been hell and they could have been spared this. Ruth thumped Colin in the arm.

"What was that for?"

"If you had told me you knew, you could have stopped me stressing for the last 6 months. I do take all the blame; I should have been stronger."

"Hay, Susie told me how Jack operated and he wouldn't have taken no for an answer. We all knew how he was with the ladies. I wish you had told me."

"If I had, what would you have done?"

"Killed the bastard."

"I knew it, that's why I couldn't say anything."

"Do we know how he was murdered?" asked Lisa.

"I hope it was painful." Said Pauline.

"Susie said it would have been long and painful." Said Peter. "I spoke to her last week. I think the police must have said something."

"Now everyone must promise never to let anyone else know what we know. Susie is banking on that. She wouldn't be the only one arrested. We knew as well." Said Eddie.

They were all nodding in agreement.

# Chapter 21

Robert phoned Flo's mobile before he left for the night.

"Mrs Sound?"

"Yes, who are you?"

"DCI Robert Downton, Dorchester police. Sorry to ring late in the day but we have a few more things to ask you."

"What, I've only just got home. Can't you ask me whatever it is now?"

"Sorry, but we need your fingerprints and it was an oversite of ours so I will send my PC to you. They should be with you around 9am, please make sure you are available."

"Why do you need my prints?"

"It's to eliminate you, as we have a few prints that we haven't matched yet. It was very remiss of me. I have got your brothers and he is in the clear. No match as I think yours will be to. But I have to cover everything, you understand." Before she could reply he added. "Thank-you so much for all your help earlier."

All Flo could say was ok see them in the morning. She put her phone down, walked into her kitchen and put the kettle on.

"Oh, dam it, tea won't do." She went to the fridge and took out a bottle of white wine. She went through to the bathroom and ran a bath. She lit some candles and when there was enough water climbed in with her glass. She put the bottle next to the bath, she knew one glass wouldn't be enough tonight.

Her mind went back to when she went to visit Susie.

Susie thought she was some lunatic and didn't want to believe her until she showed her the pictures on the camera. She wanted to confront Jack straightway, but Flo managed to persuade her to hear her out. What changed Susie's mind was when Flo told her she probably had aids. She went totally white and Flo had to steady her.

"I'm sorry I had to break it to you like that."

Susie didn't respond she was still shaking.

"You will need to get checked out. Unless you have been careful but I don't expect he would have wanted that."

"So, what now?" she whispered.

"I will deal with him; I don't want your life ruined any more than it is."

"How will you deal with him?"

"You don't need to know the details; I just need you to do one thing for me."

Susie nodded.

"When the time is right, I need you to get him to meet you at your special place. We need to arrange it so you have an alibi so tell me what have you got planned in the next month."

"I have my hen do next weekend. But you don't know our special place, do you?"

"I'm sorry to tell you I have been following Jack for some time and as I discovered what he had been up to I realised I had to act soon. Next weekend would be perfect."

"What are you going to do?"

"I will make him pay and you won't be implemented in it or the other women. I can't tell you but it will be the last time you see him."

"What! you want me to meet him?"

"No, just give him this note and go off on your weekend." Flo handed her the note. Susie read it and looked shocked when she saw the nickname, Kitten.

"How did you know he calls me kitten?"

"Because he calls all his women Kitten. I thought it was my nickname."

"What a bastard." Said Susie. "What are you going to do?"

"I told you, the less you know the better."

Flo had left her and set the wheels in motion. She poured another drink. Her mind turned to the phone call from the police, what would they need her fingerprints for? She had been very careful to wipe everything. She thought to hell with them they had nothing on her.

## Chapter 22

Helen and Karen had set off early and were almost at Flo's house. Helen's phone rang.

"Gov, were not far what can I do for you?"

"Helen I just wanted to remind you, we need to find out her shoe size and if she has a pair of trainers, but don't ask her directly I don't want her to know we are close."

"Will do gov."

Flo saw the car pull up, she opened the door, and put a plastered smile on her face.

"Morning, how was your journey?"

"Pretty good, we didn't meet too much traffic."

"Come in, would you like a coffee?"

"That would be great." Helen followed Flo in while Karen got the kit from the boot. As she entered the hall, she noticed a pair of trainers on the mat. She took out her phone and took a picture of them. One trainer was on its side so she could get a picture of the tread. She just put her phone away when Flo came back into the hall.

"Everything ok?" she asked.

"Yes, I was just admiring your trainers. Designer's?"

"Yes, I love to run so thought I would treat myself."

"Very nice. There quite new, aren't they?"

"No, I bought them years ago. I just look after them, they cost me a fortune."

"You're lucky you have tiny feet, not like me. Size 8."

"Size 6." She laughed. "Coffees made."

Karen followed her through to the kitchen and gave Helen a nod to let her know she had spoken about the trainers. Helen had heard their conversation.

"Well let's get your prints them we can leave you in peace." Said Helen.

"Drink your coffee first." Flo handed them a cup then sat at the table. They joined her.

"So, are you any closer to finding out who murdered Jack?"

"We can't discuss the details but we are hopeful to close this case soon."

"Good, I just want to forget him again. It has been awful being reminded of him."

"He really wasn't a nice human being, was he?" said Karen. They took Flo's prints then cleaned up and left.

All Flo knew was that the police knew she had discovered where Jack was. That didn't prove anything. As they drove away Flo felt a sense of relief, hopefully this would all go away.

On the journey back Karen forwarded the photo of Flo's trainer. They hoped to match the tread with the cast taken in the woods. This would be yet another vital piece of evidence. They took longer on the return journey due to an accident, which meant a detour.

Back at the station Robert was waiting for a call from Kevin, he hoped for some good news from the site yesterday.

Jess approached his desk.

"Gov, I have a result, I went to the DIY warehouse opposite the internet company and spoke to a member of staff that knew Jack. He said Jack was often seen outside in the carpark chatting to women. I then showed him a picture of Susie and he said wasn't that his fiancé? I said yes, then showed him a picture of Florence. He held the picture for a few moments and then said oh yes now this one didn't respond to Jack's advances, she just had a go at him, turned and left. Mind you she gave him a glance over her shoulder before she went around the corner. I asked him if he knew what she was driving and he said he couldn't see. I then asked him if he spoke to Jack about Florence? He said he went out to see Jack as she was such a looker and Jack said she was one of his rejects. I then asked if he had seen her return and he said he didn't see her again more's the pity as he said he would have liked to try his luck with her."

"Great, so we have the purchase of the cabinet, the sighting at Jacks work we know she had been told about his fiancé. Now if the tread on her trainer matches the print lifted at the site, we are almost ready to arrest her."

"Gov. how do you think she got him to visit her in the middle of nowhere."

"Good question, we need to see if the soil sample has brought up any clues to where he had been and if the note was written by Florence." Helen joined them.

"I've just got off the phone with Kevin's assistant, she said the soil sample he took from Jacks trainer showed traces of cement and sand so was probably from a building merchant or site."

"The DIY centre opposite where he works." Said Jess.

"Yes, so we still have to discover how she lured him into her van and what she used to sedate him." Said Helen.

"I thought about that, I wonder if the prescription Jack or even Florence was on could make you drowsy enough to make you more pliable to follow and not put up a fight. Alan, I would like you to search out this for me and see if there is any combination that she could have diluted then injected, it would have to be fairly fast working."

"On it, gov."

"I don't think we can wait any longer, Jess you and John are to go and bring Florence in, if she refuses then arrest her on the grounds of murdering her husband. I would rather she agrees and we don't have to alert her yet." Jess went over to John's desk, grabbed the keys and her bag. "Come on John, I'm driving. You can drive back." John grumbled something under his breath and followed her out. Robert phoned the local police force where Florence lived to inform them of their intentions regarding the arrest for Jacks murder and they said they would place someone close to her home to keep an eye on her until the officers arrived. Robert thanked him then turned to the remaining team.

"So, guy's, we need to make sure we have all the facts written up and checked and double checked, then, Helen can you draw up a possible time line of Florence starting from when he left her."

"Gov." Helen wiped clean the board to start again.

Florence left pregnant 4 months after wedding.

Years later

Harry text to inform her of his where abouts and inform him he has got engaged.

"Gov? did Jess say when the chap saw Florence near his work place?"

"Yes, hang on, it was two weeks after Harry sent the text."

"Cheers."

Went to visit Jack at his work

Went to auction and purchased cabinet

Week later picked up cabinet and dropped off at murder site.

When did she send him note?

Who took the photos of Jack and women?

Got Jack into her van at work place drove to
  site and committed murder by bury alive.

"You know it seems very callous of her. I
mean something must have driven her to
make her bury him alive."

"I know what you mean, he must have
provoked her."

"Do you think she just meant to scare him?"

"Possibly."

The office phone rang Robert picked up the
receiver.

"DCI Downton."

"Kevin here, got another result for you. The
partial print on the film in the camera
matches the prints you sent over of
Florence Sounds prints."

"That's great, what about the trainer? Any
match?"

"Well, no, but I would say the person has a
tendency of putting more weight on there
left side and it is definitely a woman."

"Dam I was hoping it would be a match."

"Hang on, let me finish. Florence's trainer has the same wear. I would say she could have worn another pair, unless she has binned them."

"Is it something we can use as evidence?"

"Yes. Anyway, I have work to do, you're not the only detective that needs results yesterday." With that he put the phone down.

"Helen, can you contact Jess and ask her to bring any trainers, in fact all her shoes with them."

"Wont she need a search warrant?"

"True, we have a couple hours before they arrive get on with it, then email it to the local force. They can meet them with a printed copy."

"Will do."

## Chapter 23

The   local police were very efficient and had the paperwork ready for them on arrival.

"Do you need any back-up?" asked Inspector Dick Warner.

"Thank-you sir, we should be alright, but if she becomes a problem, it would be good to know we can call on your help." Said John.

They headed towards Her home and saw the van still in the drive. Florence lived in a cull de sack not far from the main A38 route to Cornwall. It was a busy road and you could hear the heavy traffic across the back of her property. Jess was surprised they were so close. To get to her house you entered the road from behind the property and then drive back on yourself to get to the front. It was a U shape road and her house was second from the end. First impressions it was a two up two down semi-detached. Red brick with a small drive for one car and just enough room for the recycle bins. She kept it clean and tidy.

There was no grass, just a pot with a few geraniums. Jess and John pulled up Infront and headed to her front door.

Jess pressed the bell; she could hear music on and it sounded like she was singing away.

"Some ones happy." Said John.

"Not for long." Replied Jess.

Florence opened the door and the shock when she saw them was very clear. She stepped back.

"What do you want now, I answered all your questions earlier. Haven't you got enough to do without pestering me?" she then composed herself and gestured for them to come in, "sorry you caught me unaware. She had put on her game face, ready for anything. She wasn't going to lose it now.

"I'm sorry Mrs Sounds we need you to come back with us to Dorchester." Said John.

"What, don't be ridiculous. I have to fetch my lad and get him to his school."

"I'm sorry you will have to arrange for someone else to deal with it, maybe your mother?"

"How long will this take?"

"That will depend on you."

"I'm going to make a complaint, this is harassment."

"You have every right to do that, but for now we need you to come with us."

"One other thing DCI Downton, would like us to bring all your shoes as well."

"What! No... you need a warrant."

"No problem." John removed the warrant from his jacket.

Jess removed her kit and donned on some gloves.

"Why do you need my shoes for God's sake.?"

"Please can you show me where you keep them or I can search the whole house?"

"Yes, yes follow me. Don't touch anything else."

She opened every cupboard and allowed Jess to see everywhere. This woman loved her shoes. There were quite a few in their boxes like new and then there were some old tatty ones thrown in the back hall way.

"Is that all of them?" asked John.

"Yes."

"Can we look in the van?" asked Jess.

Florence looked annoyed; she had hoped they wouldn't think of looking in there.

"I only have my driving shoes in there."

"If you wouldn't mind." Gestured John. It was the same size as a small furniture van in white and it wasn't till you went around the side that you noticed a window had been placed along half of the side. You couldn't see in as it was high up and there was a door close to the rear on same side. He went to the door, when he unlocked the

door, he saw a set of folding steps which
when unfolded allows him to enter easily.
John was impressed. On entering he was
surprised to see it was kitted out like a
motor home. There was a bed settee on the
left, a kitchen opposite the doorway.
Behind the settee was a half partition which
held a shower and toilet. This must have
cost her a fortune to have done. John
started to look in the cupboard's and under
units. Near the tail gate was an area that
had a folding bistro set hanging on the side
and the tailgate was decked so when she
opened it, she could put her table and chair
on it like a small veranda. It really was very
smart. There next to a picnic basket was
another pair of trainers. Bingo thought
John. He removed his phone and sent a text
to Robert, with a photo of the trainers.
Almost immediately he received a reply to
bring the van in for forensically testing and
if she didn't want that they would send a
team down to carry out the testing in front
of all her neighbour's

"Why do you need to do this? Am I a
suspect?" asked Susie.

"Some new evidence has come to light. Do you have a car?" asked Jess.

"Yes, I tow it behind the van so I can go off to towns and leave my van parked up when I'm away."

She refused to allow them to remove the van from the drive and said they would have to do their searched-on site. John phoned Robert said he would speak to the local police and they would liaison with Kevin in a few hours. It explained why she needed another van. She wouldn't have wanted the cabinet in her precious van.

## Chapter 24

When they arrived back at the station in Dorchester, Robert was ready for Flo's obvious anger and very calmly told her that if she calmed down, answered a few questions she would be on her way soon. He obviously didn't think she would be going anywhere except in a cell, but he had to be careful as she was a smart woman so he had to be sharper.

Helen asked Flo if she would like a sandwich and cup of tea. It had been a long time since breakfast. She declined, saying she wanted to get on with this and get back so she could collect her lad.

"Have you not arranged for your mother to keep him for a while?" asked Robert.

"It, won't take that long, will it?"

"It will take a while as I would like the forensic results back and as you preferred to keep your van on the drive it will take our officer a couple hours to arrive, then a couple hours to examine and then the return journey."

"Ok, bring her here. Just be careful. It cost me a fortune to be converted. I really don't know what you think you will find."

"Just humour us. Helen, can you get a message to Kevin so he can arrange this."

"Gov." she left the room.

"Now Flo, let's start at the beginning. When did you find out about Jack giving you aids?"

"You know when, I told you. It was just after he left me."

"Didn't you want to confront him?"

"Yes, but I didn't know how to find him and I struggled to come to terms with it."

"I can understand it must have been terrible. So did you look for him?"

"No, I told you I was trying to get my head around dealing with it and I was worried about my baby."

"Don't you think you had a duty to find him, I mean he was out infecting others. He probably didn't know he had it. You could have prevented them getting infected."

Flo was colouring up; she was trying to hold on to her temper. What the hell did he know.

"He knew before he met me."

"How do you know that?"

"He told me."

"When?"

Flo went quiet, what the hell had she done. She had admitted she had spoken to him.

"I, think he. Umm I don't remember."

"Come now Flo, it's not something you forget."

"I think I need a solicitor; I'm not saying anything else."

"That's ok, we will continue later. Helen, would you mind taking Flo to the cells."

"What, you can't. I haven't done anything. Can't I sit in the waiting room?"

"It is your right for a solicitor. We can get you a duty solicitor. But if you've changed your mind, you will need to state it for the recording. We only wanted to ask you a few questions, but we are in no hurry." Robert headed to the door.

"Wait, please I will answer your questions."

Flo was almost begging, not to be taken to the cells.

"Ok, shall we continue?

Flo said she didn't want a solicitor and they continued.

"We know you received the news that Jack was in Dorset and he had a fiancé. How did you feel?"

"First, I was shocked, I didn't believe Harry until he sent the picture. Then I was angry. I mean we were still married and he had disappeared without a care for me and our unborn child."

"So, what did you do?"

"Do?"

"Yes, what did you do next?"

"Nothing, I had to process it."

"How long after the message was it when you came to Dorset?"

"I didn't."

"Are you sure you don't want to think about that?"

"I drove through Dorset and text Harry but he didn't get my message and I was home before he read it."

"Ok, did you visit the club where Jack had been seen?"

"No."

"So, if I took a photo into the club no one would recognise you?"

She shook her head. Robert looked through his notes.

"Let's move on. Have you heard of Wincanton Auction house?"

"Should I have?"

"Well, if you take a look at this is this your signature?"

"Oh yes, I bought a few things for my van."

"Can you tell me what you bought?"

"I can't remember?"

"Let me remind you, lot 364 A custom built cabinet with a false back."

"Oh yes, when I got it back it was too big so I scrapped it."

"Can you tell me where?"

"I can't remember the name of the place."

"So, you say it was scrapped."

"Yes."

"Tell me how did you collect it?"

"What, in my van."

"Are you sure?"

"Yes, why?"

"We know from the measurements it wouldn't fit in your van." Robert didn't wait for a reply.

"Have you ever been to Jack's work place?"

"I don't know where he works."

"Are you sure?"

"Yes."

"Ok, we will move on. What was it like meeting Susie?"

"Who is Susie?"

"Come on Flo, you know its Jacks fiancé. I bet she was shocked to meet you; she probably didn't believe you when you told her you were Jack's wife."

"I told you I never met her."

"So, let's get this right, you never went to the club. You never went to Jacks work place and you never met Susie. So how come I don't believe you."

"I don't know. Instead of harassing me you should be out there looking for whoever murdered my ex-husband."

Robert didn't respond, he flicked through his notes after a minute or two he raised his head and looked her straight in the eyes.

"So, Flo we have a witness that will swear in court that you visited Jack's work place and spoke with him for some time."

"They are lying. I've never been to his work place."

"Can you tell me if you recognise this van?" Robert slid a photo across the table to her.

"Should I?"

"You hired it to collect the cabinet you bought."

"I, yes, I did and I told you it wasn't what I wanted when I got a closer look at it. Why are you so interested in the cabinet?"

"It, was the same one used in the murder of Jack."

"No, it couldn't have you must be wrong. It must have been another one."

"We know for a fact that it was the same one sold at the auction. If you took it for scrapping it would have to be between the auction and the hired company in Newport." This made her look up, they had done their homework. What else had they found out.

"Do you see this?" Robert was showing Flo a picture of the garage logo that was on the cabinet.

"What am I looking at?"

"This was on the cabinet."

"So"

"So, this is the logo of the garage where the cabinet had been kept, it isn't the company that made it."

Flo went quiet, she didn't have a reply for him. She was trying to think of a comeback. This wasn't going well she thought it was time to call in the solicitor.

"I would like my solicitor now."

"Ok, Flo we will take a break. You can stay in here while we wait. Have you anyone in mind?"

"Yes." She went to her handbag and pulled out a business card, it was her boss. She handed it to Robert. He read the card and then said "so, is this your boss?"

"Yes, is it a problem?"

"Not at all. We will contact him straight away. It may be a long wait so we will bring you some food."

He didn't wait for a reply and left the room.

## Chapter 25

Two hours later, Flo's solicitor arrived and requested a meeting with his client. Helen showed him to the interview room and left them to it.

"Marcus, it's so good to see you." Marcus Miles worked in the same law firm as Flo and she knew him by sight but didn't work for him. Flo was legal secretary to the family liaison department. He was very successful with his cases but he hadn't represented clients accused of murder. The worst cases his team dealt with were money laundering and helping companies fight for legal compensation. Flo knew he would be better than a duty solicitor.

"What mess have you got yourself in Mrs Sound? Your boss isn't impressed that you are being charged with murder. Please tell me it's a misunderstanding."

"They haven't got any concrete evidence, it's all, but they are trying to pin it on me."

"Tell me what they have on you and how I can help you." Said Marcus.

Flo explained what had been happening and the evidence the police had on her.

"Well one of the first things we need to do is discredit the evidence."

At that moment, there was a tap at the door. Robert walked in.

"I would like to continue with our interview, if that ok with you?"

"Yes of course Flo is willing to get this over with to return home to her son."

"I'm afraid I have more evidence that has come to light."

"What evidence? I haven't done anything. You must have planted it."

"Now Flo, we don't need to plant evidence. We have enough to charge you already."

"I should like to know what this evidence is." Said Marcus.

Kevin the forensic officer has just reported evidence of fine syringe and remains of a subsense believed to be the same as found in Jack."

"That's probably the drugs we take for aids." Replied Flo.

"But not with a sedative." He paused to see if Flo would come back with a reply. "The same sedative as we found in your bathroom cabinet, and prescribed for your son to help settle him, I presume."

Flo was very quiet; she couldn't think of a comeback. She looked at Marcus for support but he too was stunned he couldn't think at that moment what to say.

"With all the evidence we have gathered have you anything to add? as now would be a good time."

She shook her head.

"In that case Mrs Florence Sound I am charging you with the murder of your husband Jack Sounds. You have been cautioned and anything you add will be used in evidence."

"I never meant for him to die." She whispered.

"I don't think you should say anything Flo." Said Marcus.

"It won't make any difference now. They may as well know what happened."

"In your own word's Flo." Said Robert.

"When he left me pregnant and with aids, I would have happily murdered him if I had known where he was. But as the years went by, I forgot about him and built my life the best I could. Then Harry told me he had seen him; my whole world was tipped upside down. At first, I thought who cares, he isn't my problem anymore and then Harry told me he was engaged. Well, I thought what the hell I will ask him for a divorce and forget him for ever. I found out where he worked and went to see him. Well, I meant to, when I noticed him behaving rather strangely. I thought I would watch him for a bit, to see what he was up to." She stopped to take a drink then continued. "He went around the side of the building looking around as if to make sure he wasn't been watched. I waited a moment then followed. As I got to the end of the building, I saw Jack pressing a woman up against the wall and well you can imagine. I thought she looked a bit old for him and it wasn't his fiancée. It was then that I decided I would watch him for a while to see what he was up to. You saw the photos, I wanted to find out who these women were and that was when I went to the club. I saw him with his team and the women and realised what Jack was doing. At first, I thought I would confront him there and then but decided on a better plan." Flo paused again.

"Do you need a break? Flo." Asked Robert.

"No, I want to continue, anyway, I needed to be sure the if the women were keen so thought I would have a look at their phones. It was easy to get them as they all went to the loo together and Patsy was just going on her break. So, I grabbed them and disappeared. When I read some of the text that Jack had sent it was obvious, he had a hold on them. I didn't think they knew about his aids. I had to stop him from ruining any more lives. That is when I realised there was only one way to stop him." She started to sob quietly. Marcus offered her a tissue.

"Thank-you. As I was saying. I planned it all out and yes, I bought the cabinet at an auction and had to get the van to take it to the site. I needed to wait until Susie was on her hen weekend as I didn't know how she would react. After luring Jack away and getting him into my car I drugged him and got him into the cabinet. I then went back to my car and phoned Susie. I had got her number from on of the women's phones.

At first, she didn't want to speak to me then I managed to get her to listen and I told her who I was and after telling her a few things that I knew she would only know she believed me. I told her that he had aids and he had given it to me all those years ago. I told her how he had blackmailed her friends into relationships and probably infected them also. Susie said she was mortified and how would she be able to face them again. I told her that Jack had been taken care of and he wouldn't bother her or the women again and I said what she did with this information was up to her, but I told her I didn't want any more lives ruined so, if there was a way, she could help them to keep their relationships then Jack wouldn't have won. Susie said she would do as much as she could as she felt responsible. I told her the only person responsible was Jack."

"Tell me Flo, did Susie know what you had done to Jack?"

"No, she didn't know anything. I never told her what I had done and she never asked. I think she was still in shock. She did try to phone me the next day, but I blocked her number and she gave up."

"Ok, I think we will leave it there. We will get the final details later. Helen, would you take Flo to the cells."

Helen led Flo down to the cells.

"You know I shouldn't say this but I don't blame you for doing what you did." Said Helen, then locked the door and left her to think about what she had done.

"That was a turn up for the books." Said Robert. "Good work team. Case closed."

## Jack's last day

Jack sidled up behind Susie.

"Morning gorgeous, I'm going to miss you."

"I'll miss you too. I could always ring the girls and say I'm not very well. You could stay home with me."

"No, you have to go and enjoy yourself. You deserve it. It is your hen weekend." He popped some toast on. "What time is your train?"

"5.45, if you finish work early you might be able to see me off?"

"I don't think I will finish till 6.00 anyway it would be agony seeing you leave. No, I will be strong, you have a good weekend." He grabbed his toast, spread on loads of butter. Picked up his lunch box, Kissed Susie goodbye and left for work. Driving into work he was thinking about trying to get Julia into bed again. The thought of going a whole weekend without sex was unthinkable. He laughed at the thought. Being a Friday meant he would be visiting the next site, pencilled in. It was so thrilling knowing that he had a hold on his work mates' Mrs's. Some times when they were chatting about women, he so wanted to say Eddie your Mrs's is a right one when you get her going and as for Lisa. He had to stop thinking about them and find someone for tonight. When he got into work Julia was sat at her desk. She didn't even look up at him. He walked up to her, bent down and whispered in her ear. "You know how much you excite me girl. You look really hot."

Julia pulled away from him, shot up from her seat and with one very quick reaction she slapped him across the face. "Pig." Then left to head to the kitchen.

"So, you're not feeling it darling? Never mind, your loss." Jack carried on through to the main office. There was his team all chatting away.

"Right, guy's looks like next week we are going to a place called Witcombe. It's 12 houses so I will leave you to load the vans with supply's and I will be back around 3pm to run through the check list."

"So, Jack, want to come out for a drink later. With the girls away we could go onto a club after if you like." Said Peter.

"Sounds good to me, text me with the time and place just in case we miss each other later."

"What are you up to?" asked Eddie.

"Well, I might get lucky, first I'm going for a run." He was grinning as he walked away. He could hear the guys saying he's such a lucky bastard, Yeah, he probably could get someone, but he wouldn't cheat on Susie. They were laughing.

"Little do you know guys; little do you know." He went over to his van. On the windscreen was a note under the wiper. It read,

> Meet me in the usual place.
>
> I have something very
>
> Important to tell you
>
> Kitten.

"Bugger, which kitten is it?" He wasn't sure of the hand writing but he thought it must be Susie. She had been keen on seeing him. The usual place was around the back of the trading estate. It was very private and he had met most of the women there. It didn't say a time so he thought he better go around there straight away. He made sure no one was watching and slipped down the side of the building. This could be his lucky day. As he rounded the corner, he was shocked to see Flo.

She looked amazing, this was going to be his lucky day and night if he had his way.

"Hello, beautiful." She turned towards Jack with a grin on her face.

"How did you know this was my usual place for meeting?" asked Jack.

"I've been watching you, Jack; you've been a naughty boy." She walked up close to him and ran a finger down his chest. He could feel the heat rising. He went to grab hold of her but she stepped back.

"Not here, come, follow me." She took his hand and led him towards her car.

"Hang on where are you taking me?"

Never you mind. Hop in." Jack was quite taken back on how Flo had changed, she seemed very confident. When they were married, she was his doormat. He would say jump and she would say how high.

"Here, I want you to put on this blindfold."

"Hang on love, I don't know about that."

Flo slid her hand over his thigh and squeezed it gently.

"Please, for me."  She purred.

This really was going to be a great day thought Jack, he took it and put it on.

"This better be worth it, darling."

"Oh, it will be." She started the car and pulled away. She turned up the radio and started to sing along with the music. Jack was thinking, she really had changed, he should have stayed with her.  I mean she was stunning and what he liked was she was strong which was something new for him.

He rested his head back and hummed along with the music. Suddenly he felt a prick in his arm.

"Ow! what was that?"

"Sorry, it was my brooch; I was going to kiss your neck."

"Don't stop on my account."

"The lights have changed, I can wait."

"I don't know if I can."

She laughed and Jack settled back in the seat. He was feeling a bit strange, his head was spinning and he felt very hot all of a sudden.

"Have you got the heating on?"

"No."

"It's very hot in here, I'm going to take off the blindfold."

"Ok."

As he removed it he blinked a few times to get use to the light.

"Where are we?"

"Don't you recognise it?"

He looked about; he knew this view. It was the site they had just finished yesterday.

"Why are we here?" asked Jack.

"Come, I will show you." She unclipped her seat belt and his. For some reason Jack was finding it difficult to carry out the simplest of task. His head was splitting his vision was blurred.

"Hey, what's wrong with me?" he fell out of the car. Flo helped him to his feet and started walking with him up the track. He hoped the fresh air would help, but it didn't, he was feeling worse.

"Flo, can you take me home, I'm not well."

"Don't worry, you can have a lie down in a minute." Jack tried to focus; he was being walked along the track and heading around the bend towards the field where he and the team had laid the cable. What the hell was happening to him.

"Please take me back to the car. Please Flo, I need a hospital." Begged Jack.

"No, you don't want to miss out on all the fun."

In front of Jack, he could see a ditch, he knew he hadn't left any holes. As he got closer, he saw there was a vessel lining it. He lent over to see what was in and felt giddy. He was swaying around. Flo grabbed his arm and forcefully pulled him down to the ground.

"What are you doing?" yelled Jack.

"If you sit down, you won't fall over." She sat on the side of the ditch and patted the side.

"Come on Jack."

"I told you I need to go back to the car."

Flo's voice changed from the soft sultry sounds too harsh and cold.

"You will do as your told. Get in here and lay down."

Jack was in no state to argue with her, so did as he was told. His head was swimming when he lay down. He closed his eyes to help with the spinning. When he opened them, he saw Flo lowering a lid on top of him. He tried to push against it but it was hopeless.

"What are you doing?" he shouted.

"Teaching you a lesson."

"What!"

"You've been a very bad boy, Jack. Now its time to pay for it."

"What have I done?"

"Susie." She waited for him to reply.

"Susie who?"

"Don't play games." She lowered the lid a bit more.

"Wait, Flow wait."

"What about, Ella, Pauline, Ruth and Lisa."

"Please Kitten. Let me up."

"What no excuse?"

"Why do I need and excuse, we were not together, so what I do isn't your concern."

"Is that so, do they know about your aids?"

Jack was quiet, he had to think quickly. He needed to get Flo back on side.

"Come on darling it was just a bit of fun. They could have said no."

"Could they? I heard you threatened to tell their other half's, isn't it bad enough you gave them aids?"

"Serves them right, I'm not sorry and there's nothing you can do about it." He started to laugh.

"We will see." Flo pushed the lid on tightly and started to screw it in place.

"What are you doing," he screamed.

He banged on the lid. "Let me out."

"You will stay there until you say sorry and mean it, I will be back in an hour. Then again, I might not."

"Wait, Flo please wait. Come back." He shouted.

She didn't reply.

He carried on screaming for help to no avail. She didn't mean it, she would be back, wouldn't she?

He didn't know how long he was there but he could feel the air getting thinner, he was suffocating, didn't she realise she was murdering him.

He could feel himself drifting away. Was his mind playing tricks on him, he was going to wake up in a minute and realise it was a nightmare.

He prised open his eyes wide as he could. It was dark, he tried to push up the lid, it just wouldn't budge.

The lack of air was making him weaker by the minute.

"I am so sorry." Whispered Jack as he breathed his last breath.

The end.

I hope you enjoyed my book and if you did why not read the others.


Secrets of cherry mead

This was my first novel and this is when we first meet PC Robert Downton he has come to Dorset from Oxford. Not only does he help solve a murder he also finds love. What really frustrates Robert is not finding the missing nurse, but he vows to find her.


The body in the pit

The next book we follow Robert with his first case as DCI Robert Downton. This is a very grizzly case. A young girl has a head injury and wakes in a strange room with two strange brothers who say she is their sister.  This does not sit well with the girl and she is desperate to find out the truth. Will she be able to handle what she discovers? Then DCI Robert Downton is shocked when they find a body in the brothers pit on the farm. The plot thickens

Hidden Secrets and Lies

Another case for DCI Robert Downton and his team. This is a strange case; a woman's body is discovered in a well in a small village in Dorset. The strange thing is she drowned, in the sea!

The body has been in the well for several years so this makes it more challenging for his team to discover facts and solve the case.

I have also produced 2 children's books

A dog's life

Pirate Jake

Thank-you again for reading my work, if you enjoyed it, please leave feedback.

Printed in Great Britain
by Amazon